# The Harvest Bride

## Tony Richards

**HEADLINE**

Copyright © 1987 by Tony Richards

First published in Great Britain in 1988
by HEADLINE BOOK PUBLISHING PLC

ISBN 0 7472 3085 4

Printed and bound in Great Britain by
Collins, Glasgow

HEADLINE BOOK PUBLISHING PLC
Headline House
79 Great Titchfield Street
London W1P 7FN

To Louise, with love.

# PART ONE

---

# Beginnings

# CHAPTER 1

Mallory was dead. Yes, I know that's close to the beginning of another book, but Christmas was a month away, and I was curled up warm under my continental quilt, hugging my pillow, and it was true—by then, unknown to me, Alexander Mallory was lying out there under the winking winter stars, growing already as cold and distant as they were. Dead.

The bedside phone woke me.

"Hello?"

I squinted at the digital clock. It was two-thirty in the morning.

"Tom?"

It was the first time—I stopped palming my eyes—the first time I had heard Christine Mallory sound anything other than weary and resigned. Her voice was thick with the residue of crying.

He's finally left her, I thought.

*"Tom—?"* Like the cry of a trapped bird.

"I'm here. I'm listening."

And she told me the news.

"The police say—"

"Police?"

"—it was suicide."

"Oh, God."

"I'm sorry to wake you at this hour. But I didn't know who else to phone. You were Sandy's closest friend. He always talked about the times you worked together. He thought a lot of you. I just thought . . . I thought . . ."

And she began dry sobbing into the phone, perhaps because she had just realized she did not know *what* she thought.

"I'll be right over," I said quietly. She was still sobbing when I hung up the receiver.

I sat naked, dazed, on the edge of my bed a moment.

Oh, God.

He had considered me his closest friend. What a poor, pathetic, lonely man he must have been.

Oh, God.

Then I dressed, took a swig from the bottle on the dresser, and went out into the night. I drove slowly and carefully. Fourteen years in this country and I still occasionally found myself driving on the right-hand side of the road. There was nobody else around, no traffic, and all the lights in all the houses were off, the curtains drawn. A ball of used newspaper tumbled by. A few streetlamps were smashed. The sky above was clear as glass, almost bluish in its darkness, and the bright glittering sequin stars seemed like chips of frost over the silent, frozen city. Sandy Mallory and I had never been friends, not even in the overseas years. Just two men pushed together into a shelter, a helicopter, a jeep, sharing our jokes and our terror and our black market bottles of malt. And afterward, just bitter memories. He had called me up on the phone every month, regular as clockwork, and invited me around for a dinner that he always claimed Christine had spent two days preparing. God knew why I went. She wasn't even a very good cook.

I fumbled a cigarette out of my shirt pocket and lighted it one-handed, concentrating on the road.

How many meals had I attended at the Mallorys'? I tried to count them to pass the time, but they blurred together, gray as funerals. I would drink myself numb while Mallory talked of the "good old days." Always the same stories. The golf-playing colonel. The time Jenkins thought he'd got his balls shot off. And the twelve-year-old prostitutes of Saigon. Christine would get up and excuse herself at that point, and his laughter would follow her out the room.

Alexander Mallory was a rotten little shit, a man who cheated on his wife and lied to his colleagues, a user, a waster, a weasel in human form.

Epitaph for an ex-man of letters. What, I wondered, would they write about me?

The Mallory house was a corner Victorian townhouse in a now-fashionable part of London. There were new leaded windows where once there had been boards. Plants hung in beaded baskets on the freshly painted porch. The whole thing was very tasteful. Lights burned on the ground floor and in the bedroom window at the very top of the house.

Christine Mallory was in there somewhere, and I suddenly realized I did not want the job of consoling her. I was mad to have come.

*Well, laddie, you're here now.*

Two squad cars and a navy-blue Rover were parked around the corner, by the entrance to the crazy-paved garden. I let myself in that way, squinting in the glow from the patio doors. The police, three uniformed and two plainclothes, were framed in silhouette around what might have been a pile of earth or a piece of modern sculpture. It was a human body, covered by a blanket.

Hello, Sandy.

And I looked up, and so help me, every adjacent window halfway down the street was bright, each containing watching figures, patient as the vultures at the Towers of Silence in Bombay.

Mad to have come here. Crazy.

The burliest of the plainclothes men was striding toward me. I flashed my press card.

"Oh."

"Exactly. Oh."

"You boys are here early."

"Personal interest."

"Friend of yours, Mr. Auden?"

"Something like that."

I walked toward the body. The uniformed bobbies parted for me.

"American?"

"Me? British National for over a decade."

He frowned. "I thought it was *us* lot who emigrated out *there*."

"Well," I said, "perhaps I'm just an inverted example of the brain drain. Any chance of a look?" He looked almost startled. I tried to smile wryly. "I'm an ex-war correspondent. It sort of becomes a habit after a while."

"He was one of your lot, wasn't he? A journalist, I mean."

"*Globe-Courier*. Good writer. Now can I have a look at the body?"

I should have been warned, taken it slowly, when two of the bobbies backed away. As it was, I whipped the cover from Mallory's face—and found myself a moment later leaning against the back wall of the house, breathing heavily, trembling, my eyes clenched shut.

When I opened them again, the plain-clothes man was smirking at me.

"Thanks for warning me," I told him.

"I thought an ex-war correspondent like you would be used to such things."

I loved him, too. I took a few deep gulps of air and then walked back to the corpse. The initial shock was gone now.

There had been something odd about the way the body had lain under that blanket. Now I saw why. Alexander Mallory's hands were clasped around the hilt of a slim, ornate saber. He had thrust the blade into his mouth and it had exploded out the back of his skull, propping his head up like a tripod leg. His tongue, I could make out, was neatly skewered on the steel.

"Suicide?"

"We reckon so," the plainclothes man said.

"This, don't you think, is a pretty bizarre way to do it?"

"Ritual, more like. Your friend was in the Far East a lot, wasn't he?"

"Quite a bit."

"Pick up any of their funny habits, did he?"

"By 'funny habits,' you mean like dressing

up in blue uniforms and whizzing round in little cars?''

He glowered at me.

"No," I sighed, "he did not."

"Souvenirs?"

"Sorry?"

"Where do you think he got the sword?"

It was more fine-crafted, more symmetrical than a European saber. Crueler-looking, too. Dragons and lions were emblazoned on the hilt, staring out at me from between Mallory's rigid fingers.

I shook my head. "He might have brought it back with him. But I never saw it before."

"We can presume then, Mr. Auden, that there was an awful lot about your friend you didn't know."

I stared level-eyed at the plainclothes man. "I didn't say," I answered, "he was a friend."

Even in this filtered light I could see him turning purple. He looked like a bullfrog about to explode.

"I don't like your tone of voice, Mr. Auden," he rasped. "I don't like your general attitude. May I respectfully suggest, now that you've finished your business, that you pick yourself up and piss out of here."

I glanced through the patio doors. Every light in the lounge was on, rendering the net curtains almost translucent, and I could see quite clearly Christine Mallory sitting on the armchair by the bookshelves, head cupped in her hands, flabby run-down body showing through the nylon of her night-dress. No, I did not want to get involved in that.

I nodded good-night to the plainclothes man's colleague, then thrust my hands into my pockets and headed for my car, my bottle, my bed. The watchers were still watching. The policemen were still ringed around Mallory's lifeless body. As I drove off, I could hear an ambulance siren in the distance.

# CHAPTER 2

Monday was the inquest. I dressed in my charcoal suit and sat at the back of the court while the medical examiner, the police, and Mallory's widow gave testimony. "Death by misadventure" was the verdict. It sounded almost genteel that way.

Outside, the street was full of lunchtime crowds warmly wrapped against the bitter cold. The sky above was grayish-white with the promise of snow, featureless as an up-ended china bowl. BOMB ON PARIS UNDERGROUND KILLS 60 screamed the billboard for an early edition of the *Standard*. Farther up the road a small crowd was huddled in front of a television-rentals window, watching, on the dozen screens within, French police and ambulancemen dragging twisted corpses out of the Metro. The world was going mad. I tucked my head down into my collar, and went to find a nice dark bar.

There were three empty glasses in front of me and a fourth one on its way when someone said, "Hello, Tom," and I looked up.

Robert Truman looked more like a boxing coach than the editor of a paper like the *Globe-Courier.* He was a big man, muscular and fit, with shoulders barely contained by his expensive mohair overcoat. His black hair was thinning at the temples now, but that apart he hadn't changed much in two years.

I nodded. "Hi, Bob."

"I saw you in the courtroom and I thought I'd find you here. Mind if I sit down?"

"Free country, last time I looked."

He settled himself onto the stool opposite and produced a golden cigarette case. "Smoke?"

"Personal blend. Very nice." I lighted one and exhaled bluish smoke. "I read the piece you did on Sandy. Top-class stuff. You haven't lost your touch."

"He was," Truman said, "a good writer." He hadn't personally liked the pisser either. "And how about you, Tom? Still free-lancing?"

"Oh, come on, Bob! You know damned well there isn't a paper in the country that would have me on its staff."

"It could be different," he said.

The bar was full to almost bursting now. Across Truman's shoulder, at the far side of the room, I could see a tall girl with blond wavy hair talking to three smart young men in pinstripe suits. She was wearing bright red lipstick, and every so often she would do a little sensuality thing with her tongue across her lower lip. The three men were dancing like puppets.

"Yes," I said and smiled, "it could be different. If I stopped drinking. If I stuck to deadlines. If I stopped throwing ashtrays at editors and putting typewriters through second-story windows."

"You could do all those things if you really wanted. I'm not sure you do."

"What's this, Bob? Pep-talk time for the rejects? Be kind to burned-out journalists week?"

He looked at me unperturbed. Perhaps that was what made him a good editor. "What happened to the book on Vietnam?" he asked quietly.

"It's been done before, several times."

"You could do it better. You know you could."

"Probably true. But, you know, it's a funny thing, every time I sit down to start that book I just start crying and I can't stop. It's difficult explaining rusty typewriters to the repairman."

I had embarrassed him now, and myself. What's the first sign of cracking up? Sitting down with a passing business acquaintance you haven't seen in two years and immediately beginning to pour your heart out. I suddenly felt terribly alone. Truman was staring at me with a mixture of pity and loathing.

"You used to be a great journalist, Tom," he began slowly. "The best. What the hell happened to you?"

I thought of changing the subject, but I had already passed the point of no return. Let him have it. Let him have it all.

"You know what makes a really great journalist?" I asked him. "Not talent, though that's important. Not hard work, though that's important, too. The thing that separates the great from the merely good is *detachment*, the ability to walk into hell if need be and watch and report and not get involved. I used to have that. I used to have—what did Graham Greene call it?—a 'splinter of ice in the heart.' And guess what, Bob? That splinter of ice melted somewhere on the road to Nha Trang. I don't know, I guess the napalm must've done it." I stopped, took another drag from the expensive cigarette. "Have you ever wondered why I never went back to the States, to California? Why thousands of young GIs got shot at and wounded and maimed and went cheerfully home, and I never did?"

Bob shrugged. "Enlighten me."

"Because they were too busy ducking to notice what their wonderful country was doing to them. I wasn't. I could see it all. And, God help me, there was nothing, *nothing* I could do for them." I was clutching my glass now, clutching it hard. "Oh sure, I could write articles and get them syndicated nationwide and kid myself that I was doing some good. But it didn't change a thing. It didn't stop one baby from being burned. It didn't stop one college kid from getting blown out of his foxhole."

Truman shook his head worriedly. "Journalists aren't gods, you know. We can only do our best."

"It isn't good enough."

"We do change things, but very slowly. It's a long, hard battle, but it's the only way."

"There is another way," I said. "You can surrender."

"So you ran away. You settled yourself in a foreign land, and you began to write good instead of great, and you pretended your own world wasn't out there anymore."

"That's right. That's exactly right. I don't want to fight the battles anymore. I don't give a shit anymore!"

I brought my head up and his eyes caught mine, held them. I wanted to look away, but could not. I could feel tears prickling just beneath the corners of my eyelids. Damn him. Damn him!

His gaze bored into me a long while. Finally, he said without smiling: "I think you do care, Tom." He sighed. "Oh, God, let's change the subject."

"Buy me a drink."

I sat there fiddling with the beer mats while he went to get the drinks, contemplating getting up and walking out of there. I could not. There were a few questions I wanted answered, and perhaps Bob Truman was the one to ask. I fiddled and tapped my feet for five minutes before he re-emerged from the crowd.

"Sorry to have taken so long." He seated himself. "There you are." And he looked at me and laughed. "You look like a young rookie reporter about to spring his first-ever question on some unsuspecting dignitary."

"Why did Sandy Mallory kill himself?"

Truman's eyebrows came up. "This has really got you rattled, hasn't it?"

"You don't spend two years in a war with someone without finding out a lot about them. Mallory was never the suicidal type. What might have changed that?"

"Well," he said, "there are a hundred different speculations flying around the office."

"Let's start with the most probable, then, and work our way down."

Truman stared into his own drink. "A woman."

"I ask for the most probable, you give me the least."

"That's the rumor."

"You have to be putting me on," I said. "Mallory cared more about the crazy paving in his garden than he did about his women. So how did the super sleuths at the *Globe-Courier* come to *that* world-shaking conclusion?"

"Instinct, mostly."

"Marvelous!"

"Plus the fact that he would go sloping off at odd hours of the day, then come back smelling of perfume."

I stopped with my drink halfway to my lips. Suddenly the world didn't make sense anymore. "My apologies for slandering your staff," was all I could manage to mutter.

"If you're thinking of doing a piece on his death," Truman said, "I really wouldn't bother. Journalists are only newsworthy when they get killed in wars."

"No," I said, "no professional interest. Just natural curiosity, is all."

"Well, at least you haven't lost that." Truman glanced at his watch and began to get up. "Look, I really have to be getting back. Nice seeing you again, Tom."

"You, too."

He paused. "And, Tom—if you ever decide

to stop hurling ashtrays around, there's always a job for you at the *Globe-Courier.*"

He was serious, sincere.

"Thanks, Bob," I said, touched. "I mean that. I'll keep it in mind."

I gazed at the table long after he was gone, searching for patterns in the moving shadows on it, in the beer stains, finding none. *You don't spend two years in a war with someone without finding out a lot about them.* I had said it so confidently. What an ass I was!

Which, I supposed, made two of us.

Sandy Mallory had spent the duration getting shot at, shelled, ambushed, mortared; he had been wounded three times, the last time almost fatally; he had lived through it all, come home, successfully continued his career. And fifteen years later he had punched a sword through himself over an affair of the heart. What kind of woman was it, I wondered, who could so ensnare the emotions of a callous little man like that? Was she really that special? Or was he just getting old?

I finished my drink and looked around for the girl with the wavy blond hair. But she was gone.

# CHAPTER 3

"Hey, I'm still waiting!" I called into the bathroom.

"Sorry, I'm a slow undresser. Oh, by the way, are you famous?"

"Sorry?"

"As a journalist? Are you famous?"

I considered that one for a moment. "No," I said. "Not at all."

"Does that bother you?"

"Should it?"

I could see her shadow against the open bathroom door. I shifted against the mattress.

"I want to be famous by the time I'm thirty," she said.

"As a nurse?"

"As a surgeon."

This one, I thought to myself, would never

have been Mallory's type. Too independent. Too self-assured. She knew what she wanted and, well, as the saying goes . . .

We had met in a wine bar in Westminster that evening; she was eighteen years old, a medical student, and when I had asked her back to my flat she had smiled and said, "I was wondering what was taking you so long."

Her shadow bent down toward its ankles, then straightened. If she says *tah-dah* when she comes out of that bathroom, I thought, she's out on her butt.

But she didn't. Just flopped onto the bed on top of the covers and kissed me. "Hello. I've suddenly decided I like you very much."

"Why's that?" I asked.

"Well, when I tell men I want to be a surgeon they usually make some really *awful* remark about anatomy."

"You have lovely red hair," I said, "and beautiful eyes, and a cute little nose, and—"

"You know that's not what I mean," she laughed.

"Okay. So what do you do when they make these awful remarks?"

"I get up and walk, usually."

"Good for you," I said.

I turned toward her and she moved closer, the padding of the quilt still separating us.

"Hey," she said, "you've got gray hairs on your chest."

She began an acute inspection of my torso.

"And a little spare tire around your tum."
She took a handful, squeezed. "I like that."
Then she stopped, her smile becoming slightly
quirky. She had found the first scar.

"Odd place to have an appendix," she said.

Her other hand began moving down my
side, disappearing beneath the blanket. This
time she froze completely, almost pulled
away. She looked up at me, enquiring and
bewildered.

"Go on, take a look," I said. "I'm not
embarrassed."

She sat up and slowly drew back the quilt,
revealing my legs and thighs, the mass of
white crisscross lines on them.

"They go right up my back as well," I told
her.

"Wow! How did you get all those?"

Beyond her, at my bedroom window, the
darkness was ruptured by the headlights of a
taxi purring by. It stopped farther down the
road, the doors slamming, the passengers
talking excitedly, their voices made one by
glamour and wine.

"You don't want to hear," I said. "Old war
wounds, is all."

"No, seriously, how did you get them?"

Her expression was intent, her eyes bright,
like a curious child. I remembered how close
she was to her own childhood and half
cursed myself.

"Seriously, they're war wounds. You would have been—oh—about four at the time. I was covering what they called 'the war in Indochina'—the Vietnam War. Spent two years without really getting hurt. And then one summer . . . one summer, I was heading down from Qui-Phon to Nha Trang with three other journalists, up at the front of a military convoy."

And it began unrolling in my head like a Technicolor film, as clear and unedited as the day it had been printed. Smells. Noises. My God, as though it were happening! Faces. People.

Sandy Mallory, slimmer then, with a crew cut, lolling in the back of the jeep, laughing at one of his own bad jokes. Peter Kyznik, long hair flowing in the wind, drinking beer out of a can, smiling. Stuart Rawlinson, battered-looking even then, leaning dangerously out of the side, snapping shots of children playing in the dust, ox carts followed by women in conical wicker hats, abandoned vehicles, human and material debris. He had wanted to stop at the last village's holy shrine that we had passed—the *dinh* was larger and, from the outside at least, more elaborate than normal, and the ornaments around it did not look typically Vietnamese. The delay might have saved us, but our driver had said, "No stops, man," and kept his foot on the gas pedal.

He was a black sergeant with the Marines, our driver; a grinning giant of a man. He had a "peace" sticker affixed to his helmet, and from the jeep's dashboard he had hung a portable cassette player, blasting Aretha Franklin into the surrounding jungle as though in a vain attempt to placate the NVA.

Peter finished his beer, tossed the empty can behind him into the road, leaned over to the sergeant, and said, "Hey, have you got any Hen—"

And the world turned upside down.

"We'd just passed through a little village," I told her, "called Sam Loong—I looked it up on the map later. We'd been told the road ahead was clear. So we got about half a mile past this village, and we drove straight across a land mine."

The expression on her face had not altered even slightly. Jeeps hitting mines? You're driving happily along a road, and some bastard up ahead has deliberately put an explosive just beneath the soil, and when you roll over it, it goes *whhamp* and throws you high into the air and down again like some ghastly khaki-colored parody of Icarus? To her it was something that belonged in the movies. It was beyond her experience, beyond even her understanding.

I was coming down now, in the film, falling, flailing, trying to fly because I knew that when I hit the ground . . . on my shoulders and my chest and legs, feeling the pain flare up. Peter screaming like an infant somewhere very far away. Dark blood spreading across the road toward me, from a source that turned out to be the sergeant. Smile gone. Face gone. Me, I couldn't feel my legs.

"The driver was killed instantly."

"Oh, God!" she said.

"The four of us—they got a chopper in, got us to a field hospital, but we were all so badly wounded they didn't think we'd last the night."

"And?"

"They were wrong," I laughed. "I lived; all four of us lived. They removed two hundred and twenty-seven pieces of shrapnel from my body, and then they shipped me to Saigon to mend my bones, and when I was able to walk I got up and I didn't come back. And that," I said, "was that."

"Not even a limp?"

"Not the slightest hint of one."

She was staring at my scars again.

"Do you mind if I touch them?" she asked.

"Not at all."

With the tip of her index finger, she began to trace the largest scar like a palmist reading somebody's lifeline. It branched off and her finger went with it, following tributaries and rivulets of dead tissue, very delicately, as though she were frightened she'd hurt me.

"The man who cheated death," she mused at last. "I think that's *very* sexy."

Afterward, when she was asleep, I stared up through the darkness at the ceiling of my room, trying to remember the rest of the film. Someone had been at it with a pair of scissors after that; brief snatches were all that remained, some of them not even images. The helicopter coming out of the sky toward me like some insane angel of death. A plastic mask coming down over my nose and mouth. The words of one of the orderlies: "Jesus, this guy has *had* it!" The name of the surgeon at the field hospital.

And the disembodied-seeming face of one of the nurses, a Vietnamese nurse, leaning over me, very close. I could see it now, imprinted hugely on the darkness. It seemed close enough to touch.

# CHAPTER 4

It was eight-thirty the next morning when the doorbell woke me. I came awake quickly, as though out of a bad dream, before I realized who and where I was, and groaned and relaxed. The girl was fast asleep beside me, coppery red hair splayed across the pillow like a winter sunset. The light filtering in through my window was as gray and dead as tombs, and there was frozen condensation on the inside of the glass.

The doorbell sounded again.

"All right! All right! I'm coming!"

I climbed out of bed, shivered, rubbed my hands together, found my dressing gown. I padded barefoot into the hall, and reached the front door just as the bell rang again.

"What the hell do you think ..." I came to

an abrupt, embarrassed stop, hand still on the thrown-open door. "Oh. Hello, Christine."

Christine Mallory stood there like some widow out of a bad play. Black patent leather shoes. Black stockings, ribbed. A heavy black overcoat with a sable collar. A pillbox hat, shiny as licorice, with a veil that reached down to cover her eyes. She had made herself up to look almost serene.

Perhaps the reason I disliked her, I reflected, was because she brought out the cruel side in me, made me hate myself.

"Hello, Tom." And she gave a sickly impression of a wan, tearful smile. "I hope I didn't wake you. I know you're a late sleeper."

"That's all right."

"I haven't slept a wink myself since . . . you know." Her black-gloved hands came up. She was clutching a small parcel neatly wrapped in brown paper. "And besides," she continued, "I thought I'd make sure of catching you. You seem to have been avoiding me these last few days, at the house, at the inquest."

"I—"

"Why did you run away like that?" Her voice was very quiet, the syllables broken. "I *needed* someone that night, all alone in that big house. The police acted like bastards. I needed a friend."

At least she wasn't crying. I could feel my stomach tightening. "I'm sorry, Christine. I guess I just couldn't handle it right then. I'm no good with that kind of crisis."

"You're really sorry?"

"Really," I lied.

"I'm pleased. I always thought you were a nice man at heart."

She had begun edging herself toward the doorway, but I was damned if I was going to invite her in. I leaned across it, blocking her way.

"So," I said, "how are you managing?"

"All right, now that the initial shock is over. I suppose it's human company I miss rather than Sandy in particular. And, well, he wasn't around much anyway. I'm going to have to sell the house."

"Pity."

"It was too big anyway." She suddenly brightened. "Look, Tom. When I've got myself set up, well, we've known each other for a long time, and I was wondering if you'd like to drop around and . . . Oh."

She was staring past me into the hallway. I turned. The girl had woken and was standing at my bedroom door. She was wearing one of my shirts, the cuffs flapping just below her hands. I looked back at Christine.

All the makeup in the world couldn't have made a difference now. Her face seemed to have collapsed from the inside, showing her lines, her age, the natural downward curve of her mouth. A colorless tragedy mask of a face, like putty someone had molded long ago. Her eyes were downcast, her chin tucked in and quivering.

"Look, Christine," I said, softly. "Was there any particular reason for your coming here today?"

She looked at the parcel in her hands as though seeing it for the first time. "Oh, yes. Yes. I was clearing out Sandy's study and I came across a few of his old notebooks. I've got no use for them. I was wondering if you—?"

"Thanks, Christine. It was good of you to think of me."

"Well, like I said, Sandy always thought of you as his closest—" She stopped herself, straightening a little. "Perhaps I'll see you again sometime."

"Perhaps," I said.

"Good-bye, then, Tom."

"Good-bye, Christine."

I watched her as she walked toward the lift. Her entire body had begun to sag as though under some unbearable weight. Once, at one of those funereal dinners, she had shown me some pictures of herself in her younger days. Amazingly beautiful, she had been, bright-looking and alive. And now— lost without the husband who had treated her like dirt, reduced to grabbing at confirmed Jonahs like myself. She probably knew she deserved someone better, and probably

understood that if she ever found him she
would scare him off within the first five
minutes.

The lift door slid open like the lid of a
coffin and she stepped inside, was gone. I
slammed my own door, feeling sick.

There were three ring-bound notebooks in
the parcel. I set myself up at the kitchen
table with a bottle of scotch and a glass
and began to work my way through the first
one.

*Tebbit interview. Monday 9th 11:15.*
*CND rally Hyde Park, Saturday. Check*
*Weinberger, no bullshit from aides. Nott??*

A couple of years ago. I tossed it aside and
went on to the next one, which proved to be
mostly from earlier this year, with a jotting
that read:

*Tom. Dinner—restock drinks cabinet.*

I smiled, raised my glass in salute. He had
never, I noticed, shaken his habit of doodling
in the margins of his notebooks. Stars. Spirals. Faces. Match-stick figures. These notes
took me up to the middle of October. The
last book was the one I wanted.

The change became apparent straight away.

*Belfast car bomb. 16. Blood. Jesus, where*
*does this END?*

It was written in a fingernail-on-blackboard script which had lost all its practiced fluency. The doodled stars were heavily imprinted, and jagged-edged. The spirals had become zigzags. Match-stick men, some of them many-armed, writhed like epileptics across the borders of each page. I flipped through furiously till I found what I was looking for. An address.

I was still staring at it when I felt the sudden pressure of a hand on the side of my head. The girl was fully dressed now. She grinned, kissed me on the temple.

"I've got to rush now. Here's my telephone number." She dropped a small folded square of white paper onto the table, then glanced at the notebooks. "What's this? Work?"

"No," I said. "Just natural curiosity."

What was so special about the address was that Mallory had taken the trouble to print it and then ring it around three times.

Top flat, 26 Malgarin Crescent. Chelsea.

There was a time, ancient history now, when all of London swang and Chelsea was its axis. The youth revolution, they called it, a middle-class affair brought on more by affluence than anything else. Far easier to make a living selling mantra beads when people had the money to buy them. Far easier dropping out when you knew that, if the need arose, you could step back into the job pool any time you liked. But it was fun. Modern-day Chelsea was not even much of that. Economic depression, record unemployment—these days, the King's Road had become the center of the style set. The freeze-frame society. Rebellion by pose. Boutiques and a few overpriced cafés were all that remained of the revolution.

But something had been happening there today. I saw it as soon as I stepped out of Sloane Square underground.

Just past the square, on my side of the road, a huge crowd had gathered like spectators at some deadly game. On the other side were smashed shop windows, debris and broken glass strewn far beyond the gutter. Thirty or so youths were lined face down along the pavement, legs spread, hands behind their heads; still others were being loaded into police vans and ambulances. There were bobbies everywhere.

"What happened here?" I asked one of the onlookers.

"Some kind of riot."

I scanned the blue uniforms across the street and managed to pick out, standing by a panda car, a sergeant I had known from years back. The morning traffic, picking its way slowly past, blared at me as I dodged through it.

"Hello, Ray. Trouble?"

Ray Morgan's mustached face swung around

sharply, the cheeks red, the lips pressed tight, before he recognized me and relaxed. "What does it look like, Mr. Auden? Looking for a story are you?"

"No, just happened to be passing." I gazed around at the scene of devastation. A girl just in her twenties was being helped into an ambulance, bleeding from the face and weeping. "What's been going on around here? It looks like an action replay of the Blitz."

"Gang fight. Teds and punks. Haven't seen anything like this on the King's Road for five years."

I jammed my hands into my pockets and leaned against the side of the car, numb. "On a Tuesday morning? That's a weird time to have a fight."

"This is a weird month," said Morgan, "or don't you read the papers? Whole bloody city seems ready to explode. I don't know what's got into people these days."

"That bad?"

Morgan stared up and down the road. "Half the people injured were pedestrians, innocent passersby. We've got one middle-aged businessman won't even make it to the hospital. Here, just take a look at this!" He led the way to a pile of weapons in the gutter by the side of the van. "Broken bottles. Iron bars. Knives. And what kind of bastard could have thought up this?" He produced from the pile a club with razor blades affixed along its sides. "Makes the mind bloody boggle."

I breathed out heavily. "It's all under control now, then?"

"For the time being."

"I'll leave you to it. See you around, Ray."

He was speaking into his walkie-talkie as I left. I hurried past the line of youths, many of whom were being yanked to their feet, and walked on quickly down the road. More vans and ambulances were arriving the last time I looked back.

Number 26 Malgarin Crescent was the kind of London house you felt sorry had been converted into flats before you wondered who could have afforded it if it hadn't been. It was almost as broad as it was high, a massive period house with pink and white on the facade, and tall Ionic columns on either side of the porch. I climbed the steps to the front door and cast my eye along the name cards before each bell. Several of the names I thought I recognized. The card for the top flat was blank.

I shoved my thumb against the buzzer, waited several seconds. There was a loud electronic hum, and the front door clicked open.

It was dimly lit inside, and smelled of wealth. The carpet was rich and silent underfoot. The polished mahogany wall paneling was ornately carved. An ottoman and

two gold brocaded chairs were clustered
near the wall beneath an enormous mirror.
Cherubs darted between rose stems all along
the mirror's edge.

There was a turn-of-the-century lift at the
end of the hallway, but I opted for the stairs.
Five flights. All around me the house was
quiet; no music, no voices, not even any
footsteps but my own. Like, I reflected, an
expensively kept mausoleum. I wondered why
the very rich had a hankering for such
places.

I was out of breath by the time I reached
the top, and my throat was dry. I stood in
front of the apartment door with its peephole
and its lion-face doorknob, composed myself,
and knocked.

No answer.

The lion-face doorknob was heavily smeared
with recent handprints. I waited a while, and
then knocked again.

Someone, I decided, was playing games
with me. I gripped the doorknob, turned it,
and the door gently came open.

The flat was completely empty, stripped
bare to the floorboards and the plaster on
the walls. It was all one vast room save for
two doors leading off to the left, which made
me suppose it had been some kind of studio
once. There were three small windows, cast-
ing bars of light across the floor. The rest
was darkness, shadow, nothingness.

I called, "Hello?" and my voice echoed from the far side of the room. I reached for the light switch. The fittings were still there, but the bulb had been removed.

A spider was busy making its web above the lintel of the nearest door.

I gazed around me carefully. Each window was closed and locked from the inside. There was no hatch in the ceiling, no way of escaping into the loft. No one could have passed me on the stairs, and that old lift would have made enough noise to wake the buried at Hamburger Hill.

There used to be a story current in the bars of Saigon—I think Tim Page originated it—about an American patrol who had come across a signpost, in English, in the jungle, reading, "All Americans who pass this sign will die." The patrol had laughed and walked past the sign. And were shot to pieces.

Right now I was wondering whether I had just placed myself in the same sucker's league. Because whoever had pressed the button to open the front door had still to be waiting somewhere in the flat.

I could notice a faint odor, or rather two of them, as I edged toward the nearest door. The first was a faint burned-perfume smell, like incense. The second, richer, almost coppery. Neither of them came from behind that particular door, but seemed instead to permeate the entire flat. *Worry about it later*, I told myself. I put my hand around the knob, put my left foot underneath it, and turned and kicked simultaneously.

It was a bathroom, empty save for its fixtures, with a tiny frosted-glass window no one could have escaped through. I went on to the second door, kicking it again, hearing its slam against the inside wall echo around the hollowness of the deserted flat. The kitchen.

No one there. No one at all.

The second smell, the coppery one, was stronger in there. I checked along the marble worktops and then walked across to the sink. It was neat bright chrome on top with plastic piping underneath. I smiled. Once, soon after I'd begun living in Los Angeles, I had worked for a Hollywood gossip columnist, sieving through the dustbins of the famous, raking across their lawns—I had never guessed that experience would come in useful now. It took me fifty seconds to unscrew the plastic U-bend. I lifted it carefully into the light and inspected its contents. No leftover food, no rice or peas or pasta. Just water stained with a reddish substance someone had been trying to wash away.

It might have been ketchup, but I was willing to guess it was blood.

I fished a clean white linen handkerchief out of my pocket and dipped its center into the liquid till a good-sized stain had formed. Then I folded the handkerchief carefully, returned it to my jacket, and put the U-bend back in place.

There seemed nothing more to do at the moment.

But who the hell had let me into the flat?

I was still puzzling on it when I stepped out into the cold crisp air and the light of day. I stood there a moment, my breath turning to mist in front of me. The landlord of the building was an obvious person to try, but I could already guess what the answer would be; cash in advance, a false name, no forwarding address. In an area like this, the landlord was probably a duke. I could go one better than that—I could ask a king.

# CHAPTER 5

People who hate tramps are mostly scared that, in those lost and grizzled faces, they are seeing their own futures. Put that down as one of the Sayings of Tom Auden, along with, "Anyone who hates tramps is no friend of mine."

Charlie saw himself as one of the great mythical derelicts of London, something out of a music-hall song, and perhaps he was right. *Chelsea Charlie—King of the King's Road*, he liked to call himself. Nobody around here remembered how he had first become a tramp. It was nothing to do with drink; I had never seen him touch the stuff. Perhaps it had a lot to do with freedom. But whatever, he had settled into his role thirty, maybe forty years ago, the way a barrister settles into his robes or a professional soldier into the vacant space behind a gun. He was the local character and he was proud of it. Locals who wouldn't talk to their own mothers would stop and pass the time of day with him. The restaurants and bars would slip him food and gossip. And, wandering the quiet Georgian streets like Diogenes looking for an honest man, his eyes took in everything. Little went on between Sloane Square and the river that Charlie did not know about.

He was in his usual place of a late Tuesday morning, sitting in the garden of the Drummond Arms off Ormonde Street, waiting for the doors to open so he could extort some shepherds pie. He saw me coming from a long way off, and watched me patiently, eyes hidden in the shadow of his hat. I wondered how he could stand the cold. It never seemed to bother him.

"I 'ope," he said as I stopped beside his table, "you're not planning to plant yourself 'ere."

"Any particular reason?"

"I 'ave my reputation to consider. Nothing personal, you understand."

"I'm delighted to see you, too." I grinned, turning around the chair opposite him and straddling it. I looked him up and down; he hadn't changed in all the years I'd known him. Same coat, same beard. Same string bag propped by his side full of shapeless rag bundles which might have contained half a million in five pound notes or the dismembered corpse of Judge Crater—no one had ever dared to ask. God help all of us if he ever changed. He was one of the few human beings in this world I could genuinely abide for more than half an hour.

"So," I asked, "what's life like these days?"

"You'd find out yerself if you ever took yer nose out of a bottle."

"True." I shrugged, duly chastised. "Hey, where's Billy?"

Charlie smiled. "Safe an' warm. It's bad weather for God's smaller creatures. But I *think*"—his eyes glittered, revealing the showman in him—" 'e might come out for you, though."

He pulled open the neck of his overcoat. At first, all I could see was darkness. Then, a pair of bright but tiny eyes appeared. A moment's wait, and then a small, unkempt sparrow fluttered out of hiding and hopped across the table toward me, cocked its head to one side, watching me.

"I've taught 'im a new trick," Charlie said. "Give 'im a penny."

I hesitated.

"Go on! Yer not that hard up, are yuh?"

I rattled in my pockets and popped a coin into the bird's awaiting beak. It paused a second, and then turned around and hurried back to Charlie, disappearing once again into the coat.

"That's very good," I said.

" 'Old on! 'E hasn't finished yet!"

The bird reappeared, retraced its steps toward my edge of the table, and dropped a halfpenny piece into my open palm.

I laughed. "He'd be a smash in Vegas."

But Charlie's frame of mind had changed, as it was apt to do at any given moment. He looked unsettled now. "I'd better put 'im back." He glanced around ominously as he rebuttoned his coat. His voice was almost conspiratorial now. "The world is not a safe place anymore, Mr. Auden. 'Ear about that set-to up at Sloane Square?"

"I passed it about an hour ago."

"Terrible. Bloody terrible. 'Ardly safe to walk the streets anymore."

I hoped for his sake he was wrong.

"I came down here today—"

"Bloody terrible."

"—because I want some information, Charlie."

The old man stopped and looked at me. Business. He pursed his lips and nodded.

"You know 26 Malgarin Crescent?"

"Nice 'ouse. Loaded people." He nodded, as though referring to some catalogue in his head.

"Any idea who lived in the top flat?"

"There weren't a name card."

"Granted."

"No, Mr. Auden, no idea. I know she ain't there anymore."

I lighted a cigarette. "If you didn't know who it was, why *she*?"

That seemed to baffle him a moment. He wound his fingers nervously. "It's just—the impression I got. Don't know why. The curtains. They were always drawn. They 'ad some kind of Chinese flowery design. Suppose I just assumed."

"Maybe," I said. "But you never actually saw her?"

"Not me, not anybody else. She never went out. She kept 'erself to 'erself."

"How long was she there?"

"A fortnight."

"She must have needed food, Charlie. She must have gone to buy a newspaper every so often."

"If she did, she 'ad a secret tunnel to the news agents."

"So someone, perhaps a woman, occupies an expensive flat for two weeks and never shows her face. That must have caused some speculation among the neighbors."

"You're the first person who's mentioned 'er," Charlie said. "They're not a nosy lot 'round 'ere."

Damn the anonymity of London. Someone might have been dead and rotting up there and nobody would have found the corpse until the smell got really bad. A wind had sprung up, tumbling dead leaves across the lawn. The bare rose bushes at the far end of the garden clawed at each other like warring dragons.

"Well, how about visitors?" I asked Charlie. "She must have had some of those?"

He nodded.

"Did you ever see a short man, plumpish, balding?"

"White?"

"Uh-huh. What of it?"

"No, Mr. Auden. No white men I ever noticed. She 'ad plenty of visitors, but they nearly always came at night an' they were foreign. You know, Indians, Bengalis. And some yellow blokes, Chinese or Japanese or something."

"Anything unusual about them?"

Charlie shrugged. "Respectable types for the most part. Looked like, you know, shopkeepers, businessmen." And he paused. " 'Old on, though. There was the puppet people."

"Puppet people?"

" 'Bout a dozen of them. Chinese blokes, you know, in black pajamas. I only saw 'em once—that was about ten o'clock first night she arrived. They were humping these huge packing cases in an' out the house."

"They had a car?"

"Transit van. Bright red un. With their name painted down the side." Charlie dredged

his memory. "The Sam Long Puppet Theatre.
'Cept the second word weren't Long."

My thoughts began to whirl. I gazed at the
very English garden outside the very English
pub and then closed my eyes. I was in
another hemisphere. Jungle. Heat. Somewhere
in my mind a jeep was flipping over; five
men were trying to fly, and one of them was
me.

"Sam *Loong*?" I asked, slowly. "Could it
have been the Sam Loong Puppet Theatre?"

"Could've been. Important is it, Mr. Auden?"

"I think it might be. Very."

I got to my feet, stiffening against the
wind, and produced a five pound note from
my jacket pocket. "Look, thanks, Charlie.
You've been a great help. If you think of
anything more—"

"I know how to get in touch with you.
Take care, Mr. Auden."

I was just walking away when he called
out, "Oh, there was one other thing."

"Significant?"

"Per'aps. You know number 39. There was
a gentleman called Mr. Bhardwaj. Indian
gentleman."

"And?"

"The evening your lady arrived, 'e disappeared. Just packed his bags and went."

"Coincidence?" I suggested. "He could have
been illegal."

"Round 'ere? Are you joking? The bloke

was a leading surgeon at Queen Mary's, heart specialist. The papers even did a piece on him."

I chewed on my lower lip a moment. "Are you sure he left willingly?"

"Positive. I was talking to Mrs. Corleigh next door to him a couple of days later. 'E just piled his bags and his family into the car and drove off."

The cold was beginning to bite against me now, and there was no warmth coming from inside to fight it. I tried to think of the reasons a well-established man like that would up and run. There was only one reason. Something or somebody had scared him. Very badly.

That was his problem, and mine. Charlie had forgotten all about it now. While we had been talking, a group of half a dozen small children had sidled up beside us. They were wrapped in bright fur-lined clothes like tiny psychedelic eskimos, and when the old man noticed them they burst out laughing.

He joined in.

"Charlie, can we see the bird?"

"Charlie, will you play with us?"

He stood up far more nimbly than a man of his age should have been able to, and produced from one of his coat pockets a battered wooden recorder, as though he were the Pied Piper's aged uncle.

"Bye, Charlie," I said, and he didn't answer.

His tune followed me away down the uncluttered street. It was both happy and eerie at the same time. And it formed some kind of arrangement to the two-word lyric running through my head. I could not get it *out* of my head.

Sam Loong.

Sam Loong. Fifteen years ago.

*"Hey, have you got any Hen—"*

# CHAPTER 6

I dropped the handkerchief off with Felix Benn at the Royal Chelsea before heading home. He grumbled a lot at first, waving racks of blood samples a mile long underneath my nose. "Tomorrow," he promised finally. "And I hope this isn't some kind of silly game."

I almost hoped it was *exactly* that. But by now I had realized that that was no more than a terminal case of wishful thinking.

The sky was still the same washed-out no-color as I walked toward my apartment block; the windows reflected it, making the houses on each side of the street look like deserted goldfish bowls. An empty Coke can, caught by the wind, was rattling down the center of the street. Three black kids in their early teens were roller-skating on the pavement outside my apartment building—they stopped and watched me as I passed between them, and then silently resumed their motion.

Right now I needed a drink. I walked to the end of the lobby and jammed both elevator buttons with my thumb. The first was still out of order. The second was stationary on the fourth floor, my floor; somebody was using it. I waited a few seconds, keeping my thumb hard against the button, and then swore and went up by the stairs.

I was halfway up when I heard the lift whine into action. The story of my life, I thought, and instantly dismissed it.

The cleaning service was in today. A white-haired, bespectacled old woman was attacking the carpet outside my door with an industrial vacuum cleaner half her own size, towing it along behind her like some pet baby elephant. I said hello to her as I edged past, but her head was downward, the noise was deafening, she did not even notice.

A drink, laddie, a drink.

There was an envelope lying face down on my mat when I opened the door. I scooped it up, and without stopping, went into the kitchen, snatched the scotch off the table, took my first gulp directly from the bottle. My body warmed immediately, my head became lighter. I went into the lounge, the bottle still swinging from my hand, and checked my answering machine for messages: none—nobody loved me. Then I strolled over and switched on the television for the lunchtime news.

I paced in front of the screen, waiting for it to brighten. Took another swig.

Robert Key's face came on. He talked. There was some footage. More trouble in Paris. Shootings, this time. And mobs clashing with the French police. Gallic cops in riot gear charged the forecourt of the hallowed Sorbonne. And in New York, a squad car had gone out of control and plowed through the front of a Harlem drugstore killing fourteen people, most of them women and kids. The ensuing riot had spread as far down as Columbia University.

There had been no mention of the Sloane Square conflict; it had probably been on first and I had missed it.

And yet.

And yet.

Riots in three major cities, in November? Race riots in Manhattan, now? Students arming in the Quartier Latin, now? I leaned against the side of my armchair, and remembered a conversation I'd had leaning against a police car earlier that morning. Ray Morgan had been right—this was a *very* weird month. As though everything had been turned upside down, and time had slipped completely out of joint.

The envelope was still in my left hand.

It was slim and stiff, contained some kind of card, and when I turned it over I saw there was no stamp on the front, no address or name. It had been delivered by hand. I tore it open, setting down the bottle first.

The card inside had three words written on it, so neat they might have been printed.

TELEPHONE BOX, CORNER.

I turned it over, puzzled, and then read it again. *Telephone box, corner.* Pure and pristine as a wedding invitation. Except that I suspected it was not a mere polite request. I glanced at the television screen. A man I didn't know was jabbing a pointer at a chart, explaining that unemployment was at its highest figure since the thirties.

I made sure, as I went out, that I double-locked the door.

The cleaning woman was farther down the corridor now, pushing her vacuum hose backward and forward as though she were trying some new strange kind of exercise, some therapy for aged backs and arms. It didn't seem to be doing her much good. She had difficulty straightening as I approached.

I asked, "Could you switch that thing off?"

She shook her head, pointed to the side of it. She couldn't hear. The eyes behind the spectacles were bloodshot, vacant.

"The *cleaner*! Could you switch it off! *Please*!"

I waited while she fiddled around with the machine and silence fell.

"Thank you," I said. "Look, did you see anyone come to my door just before I came in?"

I paused for an answer, did not get one.

"Someone," I suggested, "delivering a letter?"

You could, as she shook her head a second time, almost hear her neck creak. The vacuum cleaner resumed its bellowing as I headed for the lift.

"Lookin' for someone?" asked the tallest of the black kids as I was stepping off the porch onto the street.

"Yeah." I smiled. "Seen anyone come out of here just recently?"

"Sure. You." His friends had grouped behind him now. I was careful to conceal my impatience.

"Apart from me. This would've been about five minutes ago."

"Whyja wanna know?" the kid asked.

"A friend left something at the door for me. I wanted to catch up with him, thank him before he left. You know."

"It was a woman."

I flailed at the air with my hands. "Yeah, sorry, I meant to say *she*. Which way did she go?"

But I had been lying, and he knew it, and he didn't like it. He stared at me a while, his face a mask. And then he signaled to his friends and all three of them spun round and were gone, clattering down the street. I watched them go, then ran my finger along the edge of the card. Okay, I had tried and failed. We were going to play the game her way.

The nearest phone box was at the far end of the street where it branched off into Cleyborough Terrace. A glass booth approachable from three separate directions—as vulnerable as vulnerable could get. I didn't think I'd be attacked there.

Listen. Once, in Bien Hoa, I had met a soldier back from the Mekong Delta. His unit had been ordered to take a hill that intelligence *knew* was occupied by VC. It was a barren, coverless mound of earth, and he and his buddies had spent half a day ascending it, moving on their bellies, trying to press themselves flat as snakes against the ground, crawling, sweating, knowing that if the guys at the top of the hill opened fire half the unit would be wasted in the first thirty seconds. There was no one on top of the hill.

The lieutenant radioed into base and was told, hell, sorry, it must be the *next* hill. They went through the whole process again. There was no one on top of the next hill, either. Or the next. Or the next. It was two days later, by now. The lieutenant couldn't stop shaking. The men were going to pieces, saying, "Come on, shoot at us, do something!" until finally half of them stood up and ran up the fifth hill. There was no one at the top of the fifth hill, either.

But when they turned around and looked back the way they had come, they saw that the VC had moved back into position on each of the four hills behind them.

What I concluded was that somebody was playing mind games.

I pulled open the door and leaned against it, remaining outside the booth all the while, watching, waiting. There was nobody else in sight. The clouds had begun to darken in the last five minutes; there was a sudden dampness in the air, penetrating my coat and my clothes and my bones. I reached into my pocket for a cigarette.

The telephone rang, and I answered it.

"Hello?"

The booth door clunked shut, closing me in.

"Hello? Who is this?"

On the red-framed pane of glass directly in front of me, somebody had scratched a symbol. Not your average piece of vandalism or graffiti. This was very neatly, almost painstakingly done. A circle, the size of a tea saucer, composed of human heads—no, cor-

rect that, human skulls. I wondered who
would have gone to all that trouble.

Somebody was breathing, very gently, on
the other end of the telephone line.

Don't panic, laddie. Don't allow them to
freak you. Let them make the first move.

"Mr. Auden?"

"Yes," I said.

"Mr. *Thomas* Auden?"

It was a woman's voice, foreign, very soft,
almost a whisper. And yet, for all its lotus-
blossom delicacy, I could sense a sharpness
underlying it, a nameless kind of strength,
like an undertow off a calm and sunny
beach, like sharks haunting that undertow,
waiting to drag you down.

"You know damned well who I am," I
said, wanting to shout, not shouting.

"True. I think we have a mutual acquaintance."

"*Had*," I said. "You know we had a mutual
acquaintance. Just like you know that I am
looking for you. Have I made the situation
explicit enough for you? Or would you like to
talk in riddles for the next half hour?"

"I think that you—"

"Why did you phone me?"

"—are a good deal more upset than you
are letting on."

I yanked at the collar of my coat, loosening
it. I was beginning to sweat. It was an
Oriental accent coming at me out of that

receiver. Why had I known it would be an Oriental accent?

"Why did you phone me?" I asked again.

"I wanted to talk."

"Just talk?"

"Certainly."

"Why here? I have two telephones in my flat. If you know my address, you obviously know my number."

"I wanted my friends to get a good look at you."

"Your *friends*?"

"We all have friends, Mr. Auden. Even the worst of us."

"They're watching me now?"

"Certainly."

I glanced left and right through the glass panes of the phone booth. There was still nobody around.

"I can't see them."

"No."

"They're in one of the flats?"

"No. Try again, Mr. Auden."

And this time, when I looked, I did see something. Parked three hundred yards along the road between a silver-gray Granada and a bright yellow Renault 5. A van. A bright red transit van, with white lettering down its side that I could not, from this distance, make out. The windows were opaque with the winter gloom. I put my mouth back to the receiver.

"What are the odds," I asked, "that they would drive off if I made a move toward them?"

"Those are their orders. Besides, they are very shy people."

"Vietnamese?"

"Of a kind."

"And you?"

"Of a kind."

The tone of her voice had not changed once, but the undertow had grown slightly stronger.

"Why," I asked for the third time, "did you phone me?"

"You are persistent."

"I simply want to know."

And she laughed, the faintest tinkle of amusement. I had only heard a woman laugh like that once before. On the outskirts of Saigon. In an asylum.

"I think you are still a good journalist."

"You're wrong."

"The way you said you simply want to know. You would go to the ends of the Earth to fulfill that simple wish."

"You still haven't answered my question."

"I think I have," she said. "You are such a good journalist—then find me, Mr. Auden. Find me."

"A challenge."

"If you like."

"Why?"

"It . . . amuses me."

"You are insane," I said.

"No." Completely unperturbed.

"Then if you are not insane, what kind of woman are you?"

She seemed to consider that for a moment. Then she said, "Let me tell you about my mother."

"No, *you*. I want to know about you."

"I am sure you do," she said. "But I will tell you about my mother instead. You might find this enlightening."

"Okay," I nodded. "I'm listening."

"She was at once the most beautiful and terrible of women. Gentle one moment, savage the next. Her husband was the same. They lived, in the first years of their lives, in a peaceful village. A wonderful place. Everyone there was special, and strong, and wise. It was idyllic there." Her voice had assumed an almost trancelike state, growing steadily more high-pitched. The undertow surged through it, dark and strong. The sharks of madness were closing in.

"Idyllic," she repeated. "You would not believe. And then one day, one fateful day, the enemy came to the village. Many of them. Regiments of them. The people of the village were few, and they were afraid. 'One of us must stop them,' they said. 'But who?' They chose my mother to be their protector. And they gave her a very special sword. And when the enemy was close enough, she threw off her clothes and charged into their midst. And she swung to the left with the sword, and to the right, and she cut through the enemy as though they were mist. They were amazed; they tried to fight back, but such was her ferocity that she could not be stopped. This way she cut, and that, sweeping around her with the sword till she was like a storm of whirling steel. And she severed heads from bodies, and she split whole human torsos, and she hacked off limbs, and the enemy died screaming before her. And still the battle went on."

She was almost screaming herself by now.

"For days the battle continued. For days the enemy died. And the ground was awash with blood and severed limbs. And finally even the villagers could stand no more. They beseeched her to stop. They begged her. But she would not stop. Until at last her husband, in protest, her husband came out of the village and laid down among the dead and the dying, hoping that this would make her stop. But my mother was so full of bloodlust by then—that she rushed across the battlefield and leaped on top of him, and *killed him, too*."

And suddenly, abruptly, the woman's voice returned to its former deadly gentleness.

"And do you know what she did then?" she asked me.

"No," I replied. "Tell me."

"She spat her own tongue out," she said, laughing.

And she hung up.

# PART TWO

## Trail

# CHAPTER 7

"Hi, Bev?"

"Tom! Good to hear from you!"

I smiled for the first time in half an hour, wondering where Beverly Mitchell, children's editor of *Entertainment London* magazine, got her energy. She had three children, her husband had abandoned her two years ago, and she still managed to sound lively and cheerful over the phone. I was safe in my flat by now, but not warm, not even with the heating full on. It had taken the hackles on my neck a long time to settle after that lunacy in the telephone booth. I. glanced out of the window; the sky had turned black and a sporadic sleet was falling, tapping against the outside of the glass like the fingers of dead men trying to get in.

"How's the progeny?" I asked Bev.

"Bloody awful as usual. Simon's got a hacking cough, and Jessica's up to her tummyache trick again. How are you keeping, anyway?"

"Bloody awful, as usual," I said, and we both laughed.

"Oh, you poor thing. Why don't you come up to the office sometime and I'll take you out for a nice expenses-paid lunch. You can cry on my shoulder if you like."

"I'd love to. But . . ."

"Aha. Rule number one when dealing with Thomas Auden, Esquire: there is always a 'but.' "

"I'm phoning you up because I want some expert advice."

"My God, I've never been called an expert before. Ask away."

"What do you know about the Sam Loong Puppet Theatre?"

"Oh, right! *Them*!" Beverly said.

"That sounds very ominous."

"Extremely. How much do you want to know about them?"

"As much as you can give."

"Right. Hang on a minute." There was the sound of her going through her desk. "Here we are. They are, essentially, a bunch of Vietnamese boat people. They landed on Singapore, were promptly turfed off, and ended up in a camp in the States. Ohio, I think. They formed their theater a year ago and began touring, small Midwestern towns at first, didn't get a very good response. Then they went to New York about two months ago, got wide acclaim from certain papers there, though by no means all of them, and started on an international tour. They were in Paris till the end of last month, now they're here."

"So far so good," I nodded. "What makes you uneasy about them?"

"Well, technically they're very good. Near brilliant, in fact. But as for the content of their shows—I think excessive violence wouldn't be too strong a description."

"Oh, come on," I said. "There's excessive violence in a seaside Punch and Judy show."

"Not like this, Tom. Not . . . you'd have to see it to understand. All I can say is, I certainly wouldn't take *my* children to see them." She sounded very rattled.

"Perhaps the show isn't designed for children."

"Maybe. But children go whether it is or isn't and . . . oh, look, I'm sorry. I'm on my high horse again. All I can say is, as far as this mother's concerned, the Sam Loong Puppet Theatre is exceedingly bad news."

I found myself wondering whether we were talking about the same thing. A puppet show— you know, tiny little wooden figures yanked around by strings—how unpleasant could it get, for God's sake? Except . . .

"Have they been in any other major cities, Bev?"

"Not as far as I know. Just New York and Paris."

New York: two months ago. Paris: last month. Violence in both those major cities since they'd come. And now they were here. It made about as much sense as a ventilated submarine, but the connection was there; it was the only one I had.

I asked Beverly how I could get in touch with them.

"Sorry, I don't have a fixed address. I'm not sure they've got one. But they're putting on a show this evening at five-thirty if you want to go and see them."

She gave me an address in Covent Garden and I jotted it down quickly.

"By the way," she asked. "Why this sudden interest in a puppet theater anyway?"

"Let's just say," I told her, smiling, "that I'm entering my second childhood."

She laughed. "Let me know how it works out. I might just join you sometime."

I picked up my bottle and retired to the bedroom. It was one-thirty in the afternoon. I set the alarm for five and then kicked off my shoes and sprawled out full length on the bed. Put the bottle to my lips, tipped it, coughed. Save for the tapping of the sleet,

London seemed very quiet outside my window. No noises on the street below, and the humming of the traffic on the main roads seemed insectile in its softness. I let it lull me into sleep.

In the dream, we had stopped at Sam Loong after all. The four of us clambered out of the jeep while the sergeant waited, unmoving, smiling.

"Just want to take a few shots to show the people back home," Stuart Rawlinson said.

"But how are you going to take photos," I asked him, "in all this mist?"

"What mist?"

His voice was blurred by it. I could hardly make him or the others out. Thick and white as cotton wool, it was, turning the sun into a yellow smear, making the huts of the village indefinable. I decided it was a scotch mist, then wondered how it could be when I hadn't started drinking heavily yet.

"This is a very weird place," Sandy Mallory said, "or don't you read the papers."

"Come on, come on," said Rawlinson.

There were eyes, bright as jewels, watching us through the gloom.

"Hey, where are you going?" I shouted. "You can't go in there. That's their *dinh*! That's their holy place! They keep their gods in there!"

"Haven't you heard?" Rawlinson laughed. "We're newsmen—we *are* gods."

He pushed the door open and went in, and the others followed. I followed, too, not because I wanted to but because the eyes were getting closer.

It was completely empty inside. Bare bamboo walls.

"Great! Great!" Rawlinson was saying, snapping away furiously. "The guys on the bowling team are gonna love this!"

"But where's the human angle?" Peter Kyznik asked. "You tell me that."

Sandy Mallory pointed. "I think it's over there."

At the far end of the holy shrine the mist began to part. A statue was there, some kind of idol. And in front of the statue, a marble slab. And on the slab—

A corpse . . .

# CHAPTER 8

I should have taken the underground, but the rush hour always makes me nervous. The sleet was still coming down as I turned off the Strand onto Drury Lane, night had fallen, and the twin elements of darkness and ice-crystal drizzle had transformed the city beyond my windscreen into a twilight zone of blurred neon lights and half-seen shadows. The streets were thronged with silhouette people dashing home from work; their heads were tucked down hard against their collars, and every so often one of them would step out in front of me without looking, and then, when I slammed on my brakes, a dozen traffic horns would blare out from behind me. I drove at a crawl and stared out past the scything of my wipers, contemplating investing in a pair of roller skates.

I could hear a busker working as I pulled into an empty space near the piazza. He was one of the old one-man-band variety, and above the thud of his drum and the crashing of his tambourine, his strident voice was belting out a folk song.

The sky was clouded in so completely we might have been living in a coal mine. The pavement was like an overused ski slope, and when I tried to look up, spots of half-frozen rain bit into my skin. I tucked my head against my collar and joined all the other scurrying silhouettes.

*As far as this mother's concerned*, Beverly had said. There were obviously a lot of mothers who never read her review; most of them were queued outside a doorway marked THE CENTRAL LONDON CHILDCULTURE THEATRE, between an Elizabethan-style restaurant and a novelty shop selling smoke bombs and heart-shaped balloons for the Christmas season. Children outnumbered adults about two to one, and they were so excited they hardly seemed to feel the cold. There was a huge poster either side of the doorway. The Sam Loong Puppet Theatre was second on the bill.

I joined the queue and stood there for the next ten minutes trying to look as if I were waiting for my own wife and children to turn up.

"Are you on your own?" asked the girl at the kiosk when I finally reached it.

"I've always been fascinated by puppets," I told her. "Ever since I was a little kid."

She smiled. "You'd be surprised how many people are."

I took my ticket and was ushered through a black velvet drape to my seat at the back of the auditorium. It was small and crowded and hot in there. I struggled out of my coat, trying hard not to knock into the children on either side of me. More families were pouring in now. The aisles were becoming full.

To the left of me, just beyond her blond twin daughters, a woman in her thirties with short-cropped hair leaned across and said, "I've never actually heard of any of these before. Do you know if they're any good?"

"I hear they're very original," I said.

"The kids have been driving me mad for days to come and see them. They've never seen a live puppet theater. I think it's the Muppets that got them interested."

I was trying to imagine an unpleasant version of the Muppets, the death by suicide of Miss Piggy perhaps, when the lights went down. A great cheer went up from the under-ten section of the audience.

The first act was staged by a group called

Marionettes Incorporated. It consisted of a group of fluffy caricature animals, all in day-glo colors, who kept bumping into each other and walking away with the wrong sets of limbs. An ostrich and a cow swapped legs. A camel suddenly found itself with an elephant's trunk. The twins next to me squealed with delight, and I almost found myself regretting all those years in Fleet Street bars talking shop with drunks in crumpled nylon suits.

I shifted uncomfortably in my seat and concentrated on the show.

The elephant was trying to get its trunk back now. The ostrich was in an even worse state—it had managed to get itself a lion's head. The laughter in the auditorium rose until, at the finale, there was a tremendous scuffle on the stage, a cymbal crash, and all that was left was one huge amorphous animal composed of all the disparate parts. It bowed its seven heads and shuffled off quickly as the curtains fell. I joined the audience in its applause.

The lights came up a little. Looking around, I could see that there was not an empty area of floor space left in the auditorium. It was stuffy and beads of perspiration were forming on my brow.

"Do you want some of my lolly?" one of the twins asked me.

I smiled, said "no, thank you"—feeling

that slight heart tug born of lonely middle age again—and then stared at the curtains, wondering whether the Sam Loong Puppet Theatre was actually going to show. What was taking them so long?

At last the auditorium went black. The curtains rose to a peal of bamboo chimes. They had restructured the set entirely, making it look like something out of an ancient Eastern storybook. A pool with a tinkling miniature fountain. A dragon throne on a golden dais. Silken drapes fluttered in a slight draft from offstage. The painted backdrop showed a palace hemmed in by tropical jungle.

A flute began to play, its music so soft and so eerie that even the children fell absolutely silent, wrapped like spun candyfloss in its spell. The silk drapes quivered and the tiny fountain splashed.

"This story," began the quiet, reedy voice of an Oriental girl, "is called 'The Emperor of Champa's Daughter.'"

It was not the voice of the woman on the telephone, but something about the inflection was the same. I tented my fingers beneath my chin, curiosity aflame.

"Once upon a time," the reedy voice continued, "there was a faraway land called Champa. It was a happy land, a beautiful land, and it was ruled over by a very wise old Emperor."

The first puppet, a classic bearded wise man, came onto the stage, and at once I could see what Beverly had meant by technical perfection. I had been expecting something stylized, the movements exaggerated and symbolic in what critics like to call the "Eastern theatrical tradition." But the puppet was supposed to represent a man in his eighties or nineties, and that was exactly what it moved like. Small shuffles. Intimations of an aching back. Two courtiers followed him onto the stage, and one of them helped him up onto his throne. He sat there, tented his fingers beneath his chin, and seemed to gaze back at me.

"The Emperor had a daughter, Jagadgauri."

And a fourth puppet appeared, a female puppet dressed in pale jasmine robes, which floated round her like the wings of a butterfly. She moved like a ballet dancer. Even at this distance, I could almost see the deepness of her eyes.

"She was as delicate as the petals of the orchid, as beautiful as a rose, and she made the old Emperor very happy."

The flute went up an octave, the tune changed to a songbird trilling, and the female puppet began to dance. She whirled, spun, kicked and arched her tiny legs as though denying they were wood. Everything about her performance was graceful and symmetrical; not a jerked string, not a movement wrong.

"She's real, Mummy!" I heard a small girl near the front cry out. "She's real!"

And there was I, a trained cynical journalist for more years than I cared to remember, and right then I would have had trouble arguing with the little girl.

More puppets had crept onto the stage to watch during the dance, some dressed as courtiers, some as peasants, some as warriors, all of them apparently transfixed by the Jagadgauri doll. The tune drew to a close, the dance ended, the female puppet bowed.

"But," said the voice, "for all his joy, there was one thing that troubled the Emperor. He wanted a grandson, to rule the land of Champa after he was gone."

"Bloody sexist!" I heard the short-cropped mother snarl under her breath, and I suppressed a grin.

"So he called on the gods, on the great lords of the air and the rivers and the trees, and he beseeched them to bring a son for Jagadgauri."

The lights on the stage suddenly brightened, becoming golden white. A cardboard cloud appeared. And out of the cloud flew an eagle, miniature feathers carved into its wings, carrying a white wrapped bundle which it set to rest in Jagadgauri's arms. The flute shrieked three times, imitating a baby's cry.

She rocked it. The puppet courtiers and peasants crowded around to look.

"And then everyone in the land of Champa was happy, and they all rejoiced."

The courtiers and peasants danced, hugged each other, and I wondered how they managed not to tangle strings.

"But," said the voice, becoming ominous now, "there was one in the land who was extremely displeased."

The flute dropped low.

"The Spy," the voice said.

A snare drum rattled like a snake.

"The Sssspy!"

The children in the auditorium rose to the occasion and began to hiss. A pale puppet face leered out from behind the tiny palm trees at the far left of the stage.

"For many years the Spy had planned to overthrow the Emperor. For many years he had plotted, but in vain. But now he saw his chance. If he should steal away the baby, it would break the Emperor's heart, and there would be no one to sit on the throne of Champa."

The Spy disappeared. The other puppets exited. The lights on the stage dimmed. When they rose again the scene was night, the baby lay in a crib, guarded by one lone warrior.

There was a soft scuttling noise from the left side of the stage.

The Spy crept on, followed by three mustachioed henchmen armed with minute bamboo canes.

"Look out!" a boy in front of me shouted.

The guard, with his back turned, remained oblivious. The four other puppets drew closer, until they suddenly sprang on him. His wooden limbs struggled helplessly. Two of the henchmen held him by the arms. The third raised his bamboo cane—and began to pound the guard's skull in. You could hear the Lilliputian crack of wood against wood right to the back of the auditorium.

I had once seen three ARVN military police capture a deserter and kill him in the exact same way. I turned to my left, and the crop-haired mother looked very uneasy, almost rigid. The twins had their fists crammed into their mouths; their eyes were wide, as though they wanted to shut them and could not, watching machines, taking in everything.

When I looked back at the puppet henchmen, they were letting their victim drop to the ground. I almost imagined I could see a trickle of red from his wooden, lifeless skull.

The auditorium was very quiet.

"The Spy's plan had worked very well," the voice said, making several people jump. The pale-faced puppet scooped up its prize and hurried off the stage. "But he had not counted on the wrath of Jagadgauri."

The stage lights brightened. Morning. The original cast of puppets rushed or marched or hobbled into view, saw the guard's corpse and the empty crib. The Emperor fell to his knees in despair. The Jagadgauri doll separated herself from the crowd.

"She raised her arms to the heavens, and she cried, 'Help me, O gods, to find my son. Help me to take vengeance on the enemies who have stolen him. You, in your wisdom, gave him to me in the first place. Now help me to get him back.' And the gods heard her words, and were moved to help her."

The cardboard cloud was lowered once again. Three eagles swooped out of it this time, taking hold of Jagadgauri and two of the tallest warriors and carrying them up into the painted sky.

The scene changed. The backdrop was a different part of the jungle now, and it was being rolled from left to right to intimate speed. The eagles carried their tiny burdens above the tree tops.

"It was not long before the Spy and his henchmen came in sight."

The Spy was clutching the baby. The henchmen looked up and one of them pointed.

Jagadgauri and the warriors were brandishing swords now.

"The eagles set Jagadgauri and her warriors down, and at once a great fight ensued."

Blades like slivers of razor flickered against match-stick bamboo canes. One sword bit home into a henchman's arm and, yes, this time I *could* see artificial blood, flowering like a rose bud on the silken sleeve. I stiffened. There was something about the Spy puppet which was very odd. I could not place what. I was too damned far away.

The fight continued. One of the henchmen was split down the chest and fake blood spattered everywhere; you practically expected tiny intestines to appear. A woman at the very front got up and began dragging her daughter toward the nearest exit. My own weird feeling about that Spy doll would not go away. I stood up myself and started shuffling toward the crowded aisle.

The Jagadgauri doll was performing a new kind of dance now, whirling around till the sword in her miniature hands formed an orb of flashing light. Another of the henchmen fell.

I was edging my way farther toward the front, mumbling apologies, trying not to step on any hands, dimly aware of an usherette following me down. I still could not see what I wanted to see.

The battle was over, the henchmen still. One of the warriors took the baby from the arms of the cringing Spy and stood aside.

The Spy collapsed to his knees in front of Jagadgauri, clasping his puppet hands together.

" 'Spare me, O Jagadgauri!' he begged. But the daughter of the Emperor only smiled. 'You are a traitor to this land,' she said. 'You have brought only death and disaster to Champa. You thought nothing of killing a warrior and stealing my son. For this, you must be punished.' "

The second warrior grabbed both the Spy's arms and twisted them behind his back, bending his head forward. The Jagadgauri doll raised her sword, a glittering, screaming arc of brightness in the hush of the auditorium. I was three rows from the front by now.

"So die all enemies of the land of Champa! So die all spies!"

The usherette who had been following me suddenly plucked at my sleeve. "Excuse me, sir. You can't go down there." She had meant it to be a whisper, but it came out too loud.

All at once it seemed that the puppets on the stage had real ears and had heard. All but the Spy turned their heads to stare directly at me. I froze without knowing why. I could almost see their eyes glittering.

And then the sword came down.

And the Sam Loong Puppet Theatre performed its final ghastly trick.

The Spy's head popped off its shoulders like a champagne cork, flew off the stage, bounced twice, rolled. Came to a rest between my feet, staring up at me.

I had no trouble recognizing its face.

It was my own.

"Dummy!" the face seemed to say.

"Dummy!"

"Dumb and dumfounded dummy!"

"They knew!"

"They knew you were here tonight!"

"How?" I asked it.

"*She* knew!"

"*How?*"

"She pulled a few strings!"

"Strings?"

"Pull a few simple strings and watch Tom Auden dance. Watch him dance!"

"I don't dance for anyone."

"That's what *I* always said! Who's the dummy now?"

I broke out of my daze and looked up just as the curtains whispered closed. I tugged free of the usherette, began to move again. And then all hell broke loose.

Several things happened at once. Most of the children in the auditorium stood up and began clamoring excitedly. I took my next step toward the stage. As I did that, several kids near me noticed the puppet's head between my feet, and like souvenir hunters in the wake of a plane crash, they tried to snatch it up. I tripped over a boy of seven and came down heavily on my shoulder and hip, all the old scars seeming to come alive at once, burning pains flaring up as far as the small of my back, my mind screaming, "Idiot, idiot, you survive a mine in Vietnam and then practically kill yourself tripping over a child in Central London." The boy was wailing loudly somewhere behind me. A woman was shouting, "Clumsy sod! You clumsy sod!" and I think she was shouting at me.

I got to my knees, looked back, and a five-year-old girl had picked up the puppet's wooden head, was looking from its face to mine, then back again, then back, caught in a frightening no man's land between theater and reality. The house lights came up. The usherette was helping the seven-year-old to his feet. The little girl threw the puppet's head away from her and looked sick.

All courtesy of a strange little theater company from a strange little village in the Binh Dinh province of Vietnam. When I had fallen, I had instinctively closed my eyes for a second and seen the dream again, the mist, the shrine, the corpse.

I was at the stage in three more strides, on it, finding my way into the wings. Somebody in the auditorium shouted, "You can't—" but

I pretended not to hear, and they weren't about to try and stop me.

It was dark back there.

The Sam Loong Puppet Theatre was nowhere to be seen.

"Excuse me!" a voice called. "What are you doing back here?"

A woman came marching out of the shadowed corridor to my right. She was tall, bespectacled, had her hair tied back in a bun, which made her look older than her probable late twenties, and was dressed in jeans and a cowl-necked sweater. She looked busy—she had a clipboard in her left hand—and I was just a nuisance to her.

"The group that was just here—the Sam Loong Theatre. Where are they?"

She folded her arms in front of her chest. "They've gone. They've already packed up. Look—"

"That quick?"

"They seemed to have an engagement somewhere else. You might catch them at the back of the theater if you—"

I was already moving.

"But you can't go back there! Hold on, who are you anyway?"

I flashed her my press card without looking back, hoping she was really busy enough to leave it at that, and pressed on toward the back exit. It seemed almost as if they had laid human mines in my path to slow me

down. First the seven-year-old boy. Then
the woman with her clipboard. Now, as I
rounded the first corner, the next act on the
bill, eight people carrying their puppets with
them, strings hanging loose so that the narrow space was impassable for half a minute.
My fists were clenched hard by the time I hit
the open air, my jaw was rigid. It was pitch
black and still sleeting and I had forgotten
my coat. The cold cut into me like knives.

I waited while my eyes adjusted. Ten yards
farther down the alleyway, the Sam Loong
Puppet Theatre members were loading the
last of their baskets into the dimly lit rear of
their red transit van. There was a motif
stenciled onto the swingback doors, the same
motif I had seen on the glass of the telephone
box. A ring of skulls, a necklace of skulls.
Except now the grinning mouths were open.
Laughing.

The members of the Theatre worked under
their open-socket gaze, silent as hurried ghosts.

I started to walk toward them, and at the
first sound of my shoes clicking on the
cobblestones, they turned.

"Vietnamese?" I had asked the mad voice
in the telephone booth.

"Of a kind," she had answered.

What kind I was not quite sure, but they
were not typical Mongolic Southeast Asians.
Some kind of mixed breed. They were slightly
taller and less stocky than the average South

Vietnamese, with noses more prominent and higher brows. Their hair had the kinky look of slightly twisted wire. I was sure I had seen their kind somewhere before. Their eyes, jet black in the darkness, gazed at me unblinkingly.

There were exactly a dozen of them, men and women.

I began to wish I had a drink. I had brought along a hip flask, but it was in my coat, back in the theater.

My tongue flicked across my lips.

"Hi!" I said, stalling. What exactly *was* I going to say?

A dozen pairs of eyes stared back at me like dark frost.

"That was some show you put on back there. You must get paid well, what with your Chelsea connections and all."

They went back to their work. They were wearing traditional black pajamas and open sandals, and they seemed to notice me about as much as they noticed the cold.

"Hey, look—"

No reaction.

I went up to the oldest of them, a twisted little man bent by age into a question mark, and took him gently by the shoulder and turned him to face me. He was bearded, wrinkled, and his eyes had become slits. He was smiling the Vietnamese no-smile. A rictus without passion or warmth. An expression which was more like a facial mask. I had seen it perhaps a hundred times in Vietnam. Sandy Mallory had even had a name for it. The loathe-'n'-grin, he had called it. The smile of the crocodile.

"My name's Tom Auden," I said. "I'm a journalist. I live down near the river. But you already know that. You were watching me this afternoon."

No reaction, no-smile. Crocodile teeth.

"I know a few things, too," I told him. "Such as, ten o'clock sorties in Chelsea. Such as rendezvous with the lady who used to occupy top flat, 26 Malgarin Crescent. There was the smell of incense. There was blood in the plumbing underneath the kitchen sink. Do you think we can take it from there?"

Too late, I saw in the corner of my eye that one of the youngest women—a girl really, no more than five-foot-two—had slipped both her sandals off, and her left foot was coming at me. I let go of the old man, tried to turn, and she caught me squarely in the rocks.

My body couldn't decide what to do first— yell, breathe, or throw up. My insides seemed to plunge downward like an elevator on a broken cable. I started to go down, and her knee was coming at me now, at my face. I twisted, and she connected with the side of my skull instead. Someone was celebrating New Year's Eve prematurely inside my head;

rockets, pretty colors. I was barely conscious as I hit the wet and freezing cobblestones.

Somewhere very far above me, the Sam Loong Theatre turned away, and with perfect calm and quietness, began loading the last of the baskets into the back of the van. Doors slammed. The motor started.

I was just awake enough to feel an ice-cold wave of fear that they would back over me right there in Covent Garden, and then the exhaust erupted and the van was sliding away, becoming as distant as the walls of the alley.

I had died, I was sure of it. I was the very last fighter in the Vietnam War and a five-foot-two Viet Cong girl had attacked me and killed me, and now they were burying me with full military honors. I could even hear the band. Clash of cymbal. Beat of drum.

A broad, bearded young face swam into view, then most of the rest of the body. There was something large strapped to his back.

It was the one-man-band man.

"Hey, are you all right?" His voice came to me through fog. He bent closer, sniffed, and I knew that he was smelling whiskey breath, drunk's breath. "Oh, Christ, I thought you'd been mugged or something!"

His kit was still strapped on, and every time he moved, he played. He got halfway back up *(boom, crash, boom)* and stared at me reproachfully.

"Don't you think it's a little early in the year for this kind of thing?"

I rolled onto my back, clutched my forehead.

"Don't you think it's a little late in the night for sermons?" I muttered.

"Right, right, I'm sorry," he blurted *(boom)*. "Do you want help getting anywhere?"

"No. Just help me to my feet. I think I can manage the rest by myself."

"Okay, if you say so."

He reached one huge hand down and hauled me *(boom, boom, boom)* into some kind of standing position, and I had to almost struggle to make him relinquish his grip. I tottered when he finally did so, and saw the concern in his gaze.

"Are you sure you're okay?"

"Positive. You get on home now, before you keel over from the weight of all that stuff."

I stopped him just as he was turning to go.

"And by the way . . ." There was a collecting tin strapped to his front. I slipped a fifty pence piece into it. "Nice tune. You made an old man very happy."

He grinned. "Thanks. Take care of yourself."

He walked away, still hammering and crashing.

I was soaked to the skin, I ached all over, my coat was still inside the theater and I didn't feel in the mood to go back and hassle with the staff to collect it. I took a last look around me, and then began moving very slowly toward the street, toward my car. I wanted nothing more, right then, than to be warm and safe and secure in my own home, and I was glad for them that nobody tried to stop me.

Bed, my body ordered.

Sleep.

*(Crash, crash)*

# CHAPTER 9

The bedside telephone was ringing.

For a moment, I was sure that it was two-thirty in the morning and that when I picked up the phone Christine Mallory would be on the other end. She would say, *"Tom—?"* and I would say, "I'm listening," and then she would tell me that Sandy was dead, the police thought it was suicide, and I would say, "Oh, dear. What a shame," and put down the receiver and go back to sleep. It seemed by far the most sensible thing to do.

I opened my eyes, winced and groaned. Bright winter light was pouring through my bedroom window. The digital clock said ten in the morning.

The phone was sending slivers of pain

right to the back of my skull. I sat up and answered it.

A mild Scots accent. "Hi, Tom? I've got you the results of the analysis."

"Felix," I moaned, "would you mind not shouting? I have a killer whale of a headache this morning."

"We have little white round things for that. They're called aspirins. Do you want the results of the test or don't you?"

"I'm all ears."

"Well," Felix began, "it is neither human blood nor blood from culinary meats. Not, that is, unless someone has very peculiar taste."

I closed my eyes and clasped my free hand to my temples. "Felix, I admire the way you build the tension up, but could you please get on with it?"

"Okay, Tom. I think it's goat's blood."

"*Goat's* blood??"

"Now *you're* shouting," Felix said. "Where did you find this stuff? And if you say an abattoir, I'll be a very angry man."

"The less you know, the happier you'll be," I told him.

"Ah, this is your day for riddles, is it?"

I nodded at the phone. "That's exactly what it is, Felix. Riddles. Look, I owe you a drink some time."

"A big drink," he said, and rang off.

I cradled the receiver and sat there staring at the blank far wall.

Expensive flat in Chelsea.

Goat's blood.

It was an equation without an "equals" sign.

Across the rooftops, so far away I guessed it had to have come from the south side of the river, a pall of smoke was dispersing on the morning wind. I stood at my window, wrapped in my dressing gown, and wondered where it had come from and what had caused it. An office block burning down maybe. The fire must have been immense—the smoke, like some nebulous gray ghost, stretched for more than a mile. I watched a while as it thinned and paled and scattered, and then I padded into the lounge and switched on the radio to the LBC news service.

And discovered I had just slept through a riot.

It had started in Brixton and spread up as far as the poorer regions of Vauxhall. Police had battled with the mobs all night and were now maintaining what they referred to as a "tenuous peace," which meant there would be more trouble to come and worse when evening fell. All leaves had been canceled. The Home Secretary had made a statement about law and order, but unofficial sources claimed the violence would spread to other parts of the city before the end of the week.

One rioter and one cop had died.

"And now," said the newsreader, "more news of the similar disturbances in Paris and New York."

I turned the radio off so hard I almost broke the switch.

I went into the bathroom—a jolt of pain still hitting me each time I took a step—switched on the light above the mirror, inspected my face. There was a large, sore bump just behind the hairline and a faint crescent of purple on the visible skin just above my ear, but otherwise no real damage. A shave made me feel better. A liquid breakfast in the kitchen, better still.

I knew I was going to have trouble tracing the Sam Loong Puppet Theatre again; it wouldn't take much to guess that their future engagements had been canceled without explanation. But I would phone around, make sure a few people kept their eyes open.

Which left me with what?

Charlie had told me about the Theatre. Perhaps he had given me my other lead. Mr. Bhardwaj, the well-off Indian surgeon who had simply packed and gone two weeks ago. I racked my brains till I remembered where Charlie had said the man had worked. Then I went to the telephone.

No, said the receptionist at Queen Mary's, she was unable to put me in touch with Mr. Bhardwaj. He had disappeared two weeks ago and not been heard of since. No explanation. No forwarding address. Nothing.

I thanked her and walked slowly back into the kitchen.

My head was buzzing, and it wasn't just pain or drink.

Presuming he wasn't dead, and presuming he hadn't left the country, where would an Asian go to hide, to make himself completely inconspicuous? The answer came back straight away. Among his own people, laddie.

I found myself thinking, once again, about those twelve not-quite-Vietnamese and that mad voice in the telephone booth. I stared at my bottle, amber and glittering on the well-lit kitchen table. *I always thought you'd kill me eventually*, I told it. *Perhaps I was wrong. Perhaps* they'll *do it first.*

# CHAPTER 10

I had done all the groundwork. I had visited the offices of the *Guardian*, the paper that had done the piece on Bhardwaj. I had jotted down the address of every Bhardwaj in the telephone directory in the hope he had been staying with relatives. But someone had gotten there before me.

Blue lights were flashing as I turned the corner onto Brick Lane.

The sleet of the night before had been trampled to slush, and that in turn had frozen. The pavements were a glittering gray obstacle course as I stepped out of the car. Two ambulancemen were carrying a covered stretcher out of a tenement as I drew close. One of them almost stumbled, the blanket fell away from the dead man's face, and I cursed.

There was no operation in the world that would save the surgeon now. I took the clipping of his newspaper photograph out of my pocket, ripped it up, and dispersed it to the wind.

I moved in closer as a crowd began to gather.

It looked at first as though the man had had his throat cut—a bright band of red stretched across his windpipe. But it wasn't blood; it was a silk scarf pulled very tight. His eyes bulged; his lips were blue. Strangled. And the *way* he had been strangled. I looked at him again and something resurfaced in my mind like a small bright seashell reappearing on a beach.

The Marine had been crazy. I had met him in Dak To, and by then his superiors were afraid to give him orders. He had no friends, his eyes spoke of an undescribed region of hell. He had taken a liking to me and decided to let me in on what he called his "trade secrets."

"I've got my own special war paint, see. Scares the hell out of the gooks. What I do, I make a cut across my forehead, and when it like starts to bleed I take my fingers and I rub the shit all over my face. Really freaks 'em out." He giggled. "Look."

He was wearing a headband made from a

strip of parachute. He pulled it back—and his forehead was mutilated, turning septic.

"Yeah, great," I said, trying to turn away. "Keep up the good work." I was just about to walk when he grabbed me by the shoulder. The pressure of his hand was terrifying.

"I'm not boring you, am I?"

I wondered what the penalty for boredom was in this man's mind.

"No, no," I said, trying not to sound nervous. "Not at all."

"Well, lookee here. This is what I done to my knife. Standard issue, see? But I've cut barbs all the way down the blade. It doesn't cut, it tears. And this"—he was jumping around like a child with birthday presents—"this is what I use if I get up behind the bastards. Know what this is?"

A red silk handkerchief, tied in a special way.

"This, my man, is a *thuggee* strangle knot."

The same knot I was staring at right now.

The ambulancemen lifted Bhardwaj into the rear of their vehicle and covered up his face.

The exact same moment, a hand dropped onto my shoulder, pressure strong. As vicious as it had been fifteen years ago. I almost screamed.

"No need to jump like that, Mr. Auden," said a voice I'd hoped I would never hear again. "Haven't you heard? We British policemen are wonderful."

I sighed, and turned reluctantly.

"Hello, Sergeant Grey."

"Detective Inspector now. For the last five months, in fact."

"How did you manage that?" I asked. "Beat up the right person for a change?"

It was hard, with a face like his, to tell where a smile ended and a scowl began. He was short, thin, wiry, in a baggy old suit and a tie his wife had probably chosen. His eyes glinted like small hard chips of coal, watery now in the November wind. His expression wavered for a second, and then he grinned broadly, humorlessly, a ginger-haired goblin.

"Come on, Yankee Doodle. There's no need to be like that."

"No?"

"Water under the bridge. Why can't you let bygones be bygones?"

I stared past him at the second story of the tenement. Three Indian children were staring out of a window at the ambulance. One boy, two girls; all crying. "I don't forget it," I said, "when someone threatens me. I don't forget it when that someone wrecks my car and slaps my female friends around."

"Aw, come on!" Grey laughed. "Johnny Michaels was a first-class villain. He should have spent the rest of his life inside. Would have, if it hadn't been for you."

"All I did was write one piece. The rest of Fleet Street picked it up. And besides, he didn't pull the Haringey job."

"What's that got to do with it?"

"You beat the confession out of him. That's what!"

Grey just shrugged. "Me? Just thought the Jew-boy needed a nose job, that's all. So I gave it to him."

"You're a sick little bastard, Grey," I said, and began to walk back to my car. He hesitated a moment, and then caught up with me.

"Bit of luck for you, isn't it? Just happening to stumble across a murder? Aren't you sticking around? It would make a good story."

"Violent death in London isn't exactly front-page news this month. Haven't you noticed?"

"This one might be different. Expensive suit. Diamond rings. Not usual for this area. And then, think about the human angle."

"I take it those kids at the window were his?"

"Breed like rabbits, these people. But he did have a very tasty little wife."

"Go talk to her, then. She might be able to tell you who the murderer is."

"That might be difficult," Grey said. There was something about his tone of voice that was making my flesh crawl. "You see," and his grin became broader, "whoever killed her husband, went and cut her tongue out."

I stopped halfway to reaching the car door and stared back at him. The wind swirled around me, but I couldn't even feel the cold now. "You're kidding."

"The laughing policeman, that's me. Go and take a look for yourself if you don't believe me."

The ambulance was moving away by now, taking its time, no rush. The window was empty. And the crowd on the street, I noted, was dispersing far quicker than it ought. Road accidents, suicides, murders—the carnival that gathered always stayed in motion ten, fifteen minutes after the event. Not now. I remembered the faces at the lighted windows when Sandy Mallory died. This time was different. The onlookers themselves seemed frightened now.

"The kids, I suppose, are in shock."

"Tough on them, when you think about it."

"Yeah," I said slowly. "You never know, they might even have normal feelings."

I opened the car door and began to get in, but Grey took hold of me again. His grip was downright painful this time.

"Look, I have things to do."

"Oh, dear, I am ever so sorry. But before you go, Mr. Auden, perhaps you'd like to tell me what you're doing in this part of town.

Slumming it a bit, aren't you? Or are you looking for a nice cheap room to drink away your final years?"

"I'm visiting a friend."

"Oh, *him*. Yeah, Wonder Boy Singh was around here a few minutes ago. He disappeared just before you showed up."

"Peter?"

"Must be good for his poxy little paper, I should think, a nice juicy murder like this. Makes a change from police brutality or who's been selling underweight popadoms." Grey chewed his lower lip reflectively. "Didn't hang around much, though," he muttered. "Just stood there watching for a couple of minutes, and then pissed off. He didn't even ask me for an interview."

"I'd say," I told Grey, "he had impeccable taste. If you don't let go of me in two seconds flat, I'm going to start spreading a very unpleasant and probably half-true rumor about you."

"Touchy, touchy!" Grey brought his face so close to mine I could smell the oil in his skin. "Are you *sure* you just happened past here by coincidence? There wouldn't, by any chance, be something you're holding back on me?"

Now it was my turn to smile. If Grey had been standing under a falling piano I wouldn't have told him to look up, but at least I could set him a little puzzle of his own.

"I can tell you the method of murder," I said.

His eyebrows popped up like two corks. "Oh, yeah?"

"It was a *thuggee* strangle knot."

"And you, being a clever little Yank, can tell me exactly what that is."

"Didn't they teach you anything in school? The thugs were a cult of quasi-religious assassins in nineteenth-century India. They killed thousands of people with that knot, had the whole country in terror. The British finally wiped them out in the 1850s. That, for your information, was a hundred and thirty years ago."

He was still staring at me, open-mouthed, when I drove away.

# CHAPTER 11

Bethnal Green, in the heart of London's derelict East End. Every major city in the world has a place like it. In New York, it's the Lower East Side. In LA, it's the Barrio. A holding place for refugees; a place where they can sleep eight to a room and plug the leaks in the ceiling and fight the landlords and the rats until they get so sick of it they battle their way out. It was the Jews here first, fleeing from the pogroms, some of them speaking so little English they wandered around for weeks thinking they were in America, wondering why the streets weren't paved with gold, until the truth sank in. Now most of them had prospered and moved out, and the Asians had flooded in to fill the void.

I found myself wondering who would be coming after they were gone. There'll always be someone, in this crazy world.

Hunger gnawed at my stomach. And thirst at my throat. Okay, Auden, let's show a bit of self-control. I lighted a cigarette instead, opened the window a little to let the smoke curl out.

The high rises dotted all around me seemed, today, to be holding up the leaden sky. They were as gray as dying forests, rain-streaked, and they had the look of something rotting. Modern slums; as wretched to live in as all the ancient tenements round here, which still held soot from Victorian times in the pores of their walls. Black and gray, the colors of poverty and defeat. No amount of rain or snow could ever wash them clean.

I dragged on the cigarette nervously and a length of ash dropped into my lap. Grey, I realized, had gotten to me. Not with his callousness, his bigotry, his hatred—I was used to that—but with his snide remark about my slumming it. Looking for a nice cheap room. To drink away my final years. Would it ever come to that? Skid row? Or was I halfway there already? They say you can gauge the impact of a man's life by the splash he makes when he finally goes out. I found myself wondering whether my absence would even disturb the ripples on the pond.

Harven Road loomed into sight, and I turned the car into it almost savagely.

One thing about the English, they always create such beautiful euphemisms, make the dull and drab sound extra special. "Mansions" is a good word, for instance. On the one hand it's a plural noun for massive stately homes set in grounds measured in tens of acres, long graveled drives lined with poplar trees, fountains tinkling in the forecourt; on the other hand it describes a sprawling old apartment estate of the kind Peter and Mary Singh lived in. Smashed windows. Gaping, mildew-smelling lobbies. A big dog was barking from one of the flats, cooped up, probably going insane. A white kid was spraying swastikas along the outside wall.

I followed the signs up three flights of stairs to Peter's flat. The stairwell smelled like a grave.

A baby started crying from inside when I rang the Singh's doorbell.

"Hi, Mary," I said to the tired face that appeared above the security chain. "Peter in?"

"Tom Auden, isn't it? No, no, Peter isn't here at the moment."

She was staring at me out of eyes so sunken they were ringed with black, like a panda's. Her face was lined and her hair hadn't been washed for days. The last time I had met Mary Singh she had smiled at me brightly and engaged me in an hour-long argument on unilateral disarmament, which she'd won. I wondered whether I was looking at the same person.

"Mind if I come in?" I said, trying to keep the concern out of my voice.

There seemed to be a gap while she fathomed out what I was saying, then she nodded, whispered, "Yes, of course."

She fiddled with the chain one-handed. She was carrying Peter's and her nine-month-old child, Camilla, in her other arm.

"I'm sorry the place is in such a mess. If you just wait a minute, I'll get Camilla bedded down."

The place was always a mess, and she had never apologized about it before, nor even seen the need to. Peter had quit his post with one of the nationals four years ago to set up a small-circulation community paper called the *Asian Messenger*. Editor and sole reporter: Peter Singh. Proofreading, distribution, and accounts by courtesy of Mary. Both of them committed, honest people, apparently unflappable and tireless. Until now.

I walked into the lounge with its faded pink wallpaper the previous occupants had left behind. Stacks of the paper's latest edition were piled against the far wall, waiting to go out. There were filing cabinets, three of them, bulged to overflowing. And a type-writer on the scratched, unshining coffee table. This room doubled as the office.

A brass carriage clock ticked loudly on the mantelpiece.

When I looked at it, when I looked just above it, I saw that something was out of place.

There was another thing about the Singhs. They were both adopted Catholics from an early age. They took their religion just as seriously as their newspaper, their marriage, their baby girl. Never missed a mass or a confessional. Devout.

The crucifix above the mantelpiece was gone.

Only its pattern remained, on the wallpa-per where it had rested, like some visual echo.

Mary Singh glided into the room behind me, silent as a shadow. Her eyes were down-cast and she didn't see what I was looking at.

"Would you like some tea?"

"No, thanks." I smiled.

"Sit down, then, Tom."

"I don't think I've got time. Look, how long till Peter gets back?"

She shook her head for an answer.

"Any idea where he is?"

She began walking quickly toward the

kitchen. "I'm just going to fix myself a—"
She stopped, looking up at me. I had moved
in quickly to bar her way. Her eyes would
have been wide, if that were possible with so
many rings around them.

"You're not drunk, are you?"

"I passed the stage of getting drunk," I
said, "about three years ago. People tell me
that's a bad sign. What do you think?"

"I don't think anything, Tom. Just let me
into the kitchen."

I stepped aside, then followed her through.
A fluorescent strip glared against the white
tiles. There was barely enough room for both
of us.

I watched Mary Singh trying to make a
pot of tea, stepped in and helped her mop up
when she dropped the kettle.

"Don't you think you ought to talk to
someone?" I asked, wringing the last spongeful
of water into the enamel sink.

She looked up from rubbing at the lino-
leum with a wad of tissues. "Is it really that
obvious?"

"You might as well walk around with a
placard reading, 'I am worried half to death
about my husband.' It *is* about Peter, isn't
it?"

She nodded, stood up, leaned against the
draining board. Her hands kept clenching
and unclenching like wounded spiders.

"Would I be right," I asked, "in assuming this all started less than two weeks ago?"

"Ten days. How did you know?"

"I have what you might call a personal interest in all this. I've been doing a little checking around for myself."

"Perhaps you can tell me what's going on, then," she said.

"You don't know?"

"Sorry."

I tipped my head back, stared at the fluorescent light. All around me, the block seemed to hum with distant noises I hadn't noticed before: a couple of children playing, screaming at each other; a television, insanely loud, broadcasting what sounded like a horse race someone smashing bottles against the outside wall. The music of insanity. The music of a city of eight million people, and here I was searching for only one, coming up against what looked like just another hard brick wall.

Go back to war reporting, laddie, I told myself. It's easier.

Mary was staring at me anxiously.

"Just suppose," I said, "you tell me exactly what you do know?"

She stared at her hands, then folded them across her breasts as though to stop them from moving. They remained fidgety all the same.

"It didn't really start with Peter," she began, talking slowly, trying to keep everything in sequence. "It was just—a tightening up in the community."

"The Asian community?"

"Peter came home one day, very worried, upset almost. Everyone around here's always trusted him, confided in him, even though he's a Christian. They knew he was a good and educated man who was out to help them, so they opened up to him. He used to boast"—and she smiled a little despite herself—"that when a child in the area got new shoes, he was always among the first to know about it. Then, overnight, everything changed. Oh, he still got to hear about the new shoes, the little things, but he knew people were holding something back from him. Good journalists have that kind of instinct, don't they?"

"Uh-huh." I nodded, chewing at my thumb. I knew exactly how it was. You strike up a special relationship with, say, a politician, and he buys you drinks and jokes with you and slips you bits of inside information, and then all of a sudden the drinking sessions become shorter, the smiles become false, and you *know* that he's a liar by default, that there's something going on he doesn't want you or anybody else to know about. It is a bad, let-down feeling. It burns like ... like napalm.

"He was very, very low. He brooded on it all night, seemed to have the idea they were excluding him for the one reason they never had, because of his religion. Anyway, being a good reporter, he went out poking around the next day. Didn't find anything, but they knew he was suspicious. That evening three of the community elders came around. They said something to him, and he sent me out of the room, the first time he's ever done that. I tried to listen through the door. They were talking in Bengali; Peter speaks it, but I never bothered to learn. Around nine o'clock, all four of them left. Peter didn't come home till midnight, and he wouldn't tell me what was going on.

"The next evening, he disappeared again. And the next. You know"—she laughed nervously—"under any other circumstances, I might have believed he was seeing another woman."

I grinned along with her, not letting on how close to the truth she had probably come.

"The crucifix vanished," she said. "I'm sure you noticed that."

"Eagle-Eye Auden," I said, "that's me."

"And he used to wear a cross around his neck. That's gone, too. He's replaced it with some horrible amulet. It's a round thing, made of bronze. It has this strange pattern on it, human skulls set in a ring. When I first saw it I nearly threw a fit. I tried to drag it off him and—"

She paused a long while this time. There were tears welling in the corners of her eyes.

"And?"

"He hit me. Punched me in the stomach. He's never, ever done anything . . . like that." She buried her face in her hands. She breathed in deeply, snorting, fighting to control herself. I thought of putting an arm around her, but it was the last thing she needed right now. "I'm sorry," she said at last. "I don't think, even now, it's properly sunk in."

The walls of the kitchen seemed horribly close. There was nowhere else to look but at her anguished face. God, if only they had some alcohol in this place! "You've no idea at all," I asked, "why he's behaving this way?"

"I've tried to talk to him about it, how many times I can't remember. He just looks blank or says 'trust me.' You know, as in: I am the head of this household; I am doing all this for the good of my wife and child. That's what he implies."

"And you're positive you don't know where he is? It's important, Mary. Like I said, I've got an interest in this, too."

Her features smoothed out a little, became

thoughtful, part of the old Mary Singh returning to the surface. "There was one thing. One of the elders who came round here the first time, he's lived here about thirty years, owns a greengrocer's chain. He used to have a warehouse in the old docks. And each time Peter's come back this last week he's smelled of—I don't know what it could be—stagnant mud? There was mud all over the car as well."

"Where is the warehouse, Mary?" I asked.

"I'm not sure. Somewhere near the Woolwich Ferry, I think, on the north bank. Directly on the river. It seems such a long shot."

"Worth a try," I reassured her.

I got the name of the elder and of his firm, but there seemed little else she could give me. Except to warn me to be careful.

"If I'm not back in two hours," I told her, "put in a call to a Detective Inspector Grey."

"He'll help?"

"No, he'll celebrate. But if I'm going to go out, I might as well make someone happy."

The swastika-spraying hooligan was gone when I walked out to the car. I wondered what he'd have done if he knew the swastika was an ancient Sanskrit symbol, created by the Indians themselves, a sign of peace.

I was on form today. Tom Auden, purveyor of useless information. Swastikas, *thuggee* knots, religious devices as powerful and strange as the mark left by that missing cross. I found myself wishing I knew a little more about the thug cult. Perhaps Peter Singh could tell me.

Shopkeepers were boarding up their windows as I drove away from Bethnal Green. They had heard about the riots, too. Nobody was taking any chances.

# CHAPTER 12

The name of the warehouse owner was K. J. Gopali. His name was painted on the doors in huge, flaking green letters when I finally arrived. It was getting dark now. And the skies, as though fulfilling a promise they'd reneged on a dozen times, had begun to gently snow. At any other time, any place in the world, children by the thousand would be standing by their garden windows now, watching the stuff collect, planning all the games they would play the following morning. I suspected, if things kept going the way they were, the streets would not be safe by tomorrow dawn.

Peter's battered gray Cortina was parked by the side of the warehouse along with half a dozen other cars. One of them was the red transit van. I swung my own car around in the wide, slimy cobbled yard out front, parked it in the shadow of another warehouse farther down, and killed the lights. There was a bottle of scotch with me now; I'd picked it up on the way here. I emptied it a little, let the amber fluid do its work, then stepped out of the car.

But no amount of alcohol in the world could make the twilit docklands seem anything less than macabre. Once this place was the heart of commercial London; the city's very lifeblood flowed here. There is nothing quieter, more unnerving, than a heart that has stopped beating. Great empty buildings loomed at me from all around, their timbers rotting, their jagged-edged windows gaping like dead mouths. Occasionally a piece of canvas would flap, or something would creak, and though I'm not a gambling man I'd be willing to bet my savings even Vlad the Impaler would have been afraid. A boat sounded its horn far away down the bend of the river. There was a distant thrum of traffic from the far bank, a galaxy of tiny lights where the shops were just shutting up and people were going home to their families, their television sets, their central heating.

No use invoking the old metaphor of a man sinking in a marsh on the moors, watching the lights of a sleepy village several miles away. I had felt like that for the past fifteen years.

I began walking toward the warehouse. The snow came with me, collecting on me like an affectionate white friend.

There had been a small wharf at the front of the warehouse. It had collapsed, and so had all the pilings right along the bank. The river was at high tide now; it lapped up the cobblestones almost to the enormous warehouse doors, throwing up a scum of weed and driftwood and empty plastic bottles. The smell was like a sewage farm; I didn't wonder Mary Singh had noticed it on Peter. The warehouse itself was built of corrugated iron, thickly painted once, blotched through with rust now. The doors themselves were big enough to let a loaded truck in, but there was a smaller hatch in one of them, human-sized. I was damned if I would walk in through the front entrance. I tried around the side.

"You're a very talented kid," the editor of my first newspaper job had said to me.

"I like to think so, sir."

"Then, let me give you some advice."

"Why not? Everyone else has." Cocky, even at that age.

"In people like yourself, there's two separate entities. The human being, and the talent. And the talent hates the human being because the human being's weak. It has to sleep, it has to eat, it hurts, it insists on going to the can when the talent wants to keep on working. So, the talent tries to destroy it. Might be dope—look at Billie Holiday. Might be fast driving. Might be booze. You don't have to look much farther than this office to know about booze and, Christ, we're just a little outfit in the sticks. The point is, the talent keeps on trying. And if nothing else works, you know what it tries?"

"No. What?"

"It takes the human being by the scruff of the neck and jams him into the worst, most dangerous situations it can find. Hemingway, for Christ's sake! Look what that bastard kept doing to himself!"

"So what you're telling me," I said, "is to take care of myself and ignore the wicked talent."

"No, I'm not telling you exactly that. You have to give the talent leeway or it shrivels up and dies, the human being ends up killing it. Just always be aware of what it tries to do to you, and keep it under control."

I wondered whether it was that, the monster talent, that had led me to Vietnam and was leading me to this place now. I'd never thought of myself as someone with a death wish. Right here, among the grave-quiet docks, it wasn't a particularly consoling idea.

I found the side entrance. It was a cobbled-together wooden door, and when I eased it open a rat scampered across my shoes. The sun was nine-tenths gone by now. The light was almost nonexistent, and I heard the noises inside the building long before my eyes adjusted. Human voices, intoning in a language I had never heard before. And a weird ethereal moaning noise I could have listened to for hours without guessing what it was. The only way onward, I finally saw, was up a flight of rickety stairs that looked like someone had been playing with match sticks and a tube of glue. At the foot of the stairs was a statue of an Eastern stylized demon-dog. I patted it gently on the head, and then slipped off my shoes and began to climb.

I couldn't see much, which was perhaps just as well since what I *could* see I didn't much like. I was in a wooden gallery which ran the whole circumference of the building. There was another flight of stairs down to the floor, but I didn't feel like using them at that particular moment.

There was a congregation of about fifty people down below, dimly lit by candles, kneeling, pooled together by their own shadows. In front of them, an altar, an idol, and a grisly frieze at the very back. The idol was in silhouette, and I could only make out that it was standing, perhaps dancing, and that it had four arms. They held a sword, a shield, a noose, and something that might have been a severed human head. The frieze was more distinct. It showed four—a magic number? —dead or dying men. One was being strangled by a skeleton. One being impaled. One being crushed to death by a hag. Who also was merrily decapitating the fourth. A cowled priest stood before the altar, as distinguishably human as a short black pencil stub. Kneeling in front of him was Peter.

There was a lot of wailing and chanting going on. Something large and shapeless and unmoving was lying on the altar. Next to that, a bowl which gleamed dull bronze in the candlelight. The priest picked up the bowl, dipped his fingers into it, worked with them at Peter's forehead.

I was witnessing a baptism, and I supposed I could guess what was in the bowl. I sat down in the shadows, not wanting to watch any more, and waited for the ceremony to end.

That moaning noise, I realized, was the wind. It had gotten into the warehouse somehow, but it seemed to be remaining downstairs, as though someone had sent it an invitation card. I let it fill my consciousness, watched the flickering candlelight throw nice, pretty patterns on the wooden rails in front of me. God, I needed something pretty right now.

Peter remained behind when the rest of them finally stood and filed away. He was still kneeling in front of the altar, but now his shoulders were heaving up and down. Crying, being ill, it made no difference; no one throws away the beliefs of a lifetime without some degree of pain. I hoped that would work in my favor.

I bided my time till I heard the last of the cars drive away. Then I stood up, leaned over the balcony and said, "Hello, Peter."

He looked around.

"Suppose," I said, "we have a talk about your nice new friends."

He was watching me, still kneeling, as I came down the stairs, slipping my shoes on as I walked. His eyes were wide and bright and his cheeks glistened damply. The design on his forehead was a skull; some of the blood had dribbled down the side of his nose right to his lips but he seemed oblivious of it.

The smell down here was the same as in the Chelsea flat. Burned perfume and copper. Incense and blood. The shapeless object on the altar was a goat with its throat cut.

Peter's mouth worked uncertainly.

"Lost for words?" I asked. "That's not like you."

"Go away, Tom. You are a fool."

"Perhaps." I yanked at one of the goat's

legs and it tumbled down in front of him like a sack. "What would your priest say if he knew about all this?"

"Don't talk to me like a child."

"Isn't that what children do? Play around with dirt?"

"It doesn't matter what my priest thinks."

"No?"

"I've," and he almost grinned, "converted."

"To what?"

"The winning side."

I took a step toward him; it seemed to echo forever and ever. I could almost hear my heart beat. The wind seemed louder now that the chanting had stopped. It was like a live thing, prowling the corners of the warehouse, waiting for its chance.

"Oh, I'm sorry," I said. "I didn't know there *were* sides, much less that one of them was already claiming victory. What is this, Peter? A war?"

He shrugged, then said, "How did you find me? How did you know about this place?"

"I have the right to protect my sources. You know that."

"Mary?"

I sighed. "What the fuck do you think, Peter?"

"When I get home—"

"She's *concerned* about you, idiot. Besides, what makes you think you're going to get home?"

Peter stared at me as though I'd just announced the arrival of men from the moon.

"We are friends," he said.

"*Were* friends. I'm getting a little fed up with all this. I've been chasing all over London these past few days and I want to know exactly why. I also want to know why a surgeon called Bhardwaj is dead."

He didn't reply. I don't think he could.

"Did you kill Bhardwaj?" I asked him.

He closed his eyes.

"Did you? Did you have fun ripping the tongue out of his wife? How about his kids? They must have *loved* watching you at work. Did they scream a lot? Or did you slap them around until they shut up, a big wonderful deeply religious man like you?"

"I was the lookout only. There had to be a price." He would not open his eyes. His voice sounded like something being dragged out of a pit.

"A high price, don't you think?" I said.

"Yes. I am not proud of what happened."

"And what do you get in return, apart from a faceful of blood?"

The wind moaned and I looked around. Something Charlie had said came back to me. *The curtains. They were always drawn. They 'ad some kind of Chinese flowery design.* There were screens all round the temple like a second wall. The design was flowers, thorned blooms, curling from the mouths of stylized monsters. The eyes of the monsters seemed to watch me.

"Safety," Peter was saying. "For me. For my family. You really don't understand what's going on, do you."

"Uh-uh. Not little me."

"She's here. She's come to the West."

"The woman?" I asked, sick of his riddles.

And at last he opened his eyes. The look he gave me now was one of almost pity.

"No," he whispered, shaking his head, "you don't understand at all, Tom."

The wind suddenly gusted.

The candles blew out.

I could not see my hand in front of my face. Dimly through my panic, I heard Peter getting to his feet.

"I have a knife, Tom."

I could tell from his voice that he was not lying. I tried to swallow, and then gave it up as a bad job. "This'll be fun," I said. "Pin the donkey in the dark."

"Always so calm, Tom."

"All right, my hands are shaking! I'm terrified! Is that what you want me to say, cause it's true!" Something in me wanted to reach out, try and get hold of him, but it didn't take much to guess what the outcome would be. "You might hurt yourself with that thing," I told him as calmly as I could.

"I am baptized now. I am protected. She will guide me to you if the need arises."

"Who's *she*, if it's not the woman?"

"Still questions, Tom? Even now?" There was still the catch of tears in his voice. "I will make a bargain with you."

"Fine. Good. Bargain away."

"You will not follow me back to my flat. You will not speak to me or my wife again. You will leave us alone. In return, I will give you your life."

"What if I go to the police?"

"I know you. I don't think you will just yet."

"And besides, you wouldn't tell them anything, would you?"

"No."

"Unlike Bhardwaj, who might just have decided to speak out."

I could practically hear him quivering in the darkness. Any moment now, and his shoulders would start heaving again.

"I'm going now, Tom," he whispered.

"Good-bye, Peter." I waited till he had taken the first few steps, and then I called out, "Peter!" and he stopped.

"I'm remembering something you first said," I told him, "when you quit your regular job to found the *Messenger*. You said, 'I'm not going to stand for causes, Tom, just for individual people, individual rights. If I can't get my own way without hurting one of my people, I won't do it.'" I frowned, wishing he could see it. "The man who said that, Peter, died this evening."

I stood alone in the darkness a long while after he had gone, seeing nothing, thinking too much. Then, finally, I got out my lighter and thumbed on the flame. I turned back to the altar, took a closer look at the idol.

It wasn't the fact that it was a woman that made me stiffen. It wasn't the belt of human hands it was wearing, or even the necklace of skulls around its throat.

I held the lighter higher. The butane glow flickered around the idol's face.

# CHAPTER 13

The answering machine was holding a message when I got home. I ran it back and played it.

"Tom," said Bob Truman's voice. "Something's just come up which might interest you. About Sandy Mallory. Give me a buzz as soon as you can, okay?"

I tried the *Globe-Courier* offices first, got the night staff. No, Bob had packed up half an hour ago. Did I want to leave a message?

I picked through pieces of scrap paper, jottings on the backs of envelopes, until I found his home number. I began to dial, hoping to God he hadn't gone out.

His twelve-year-old daughter answered the phone and Bob was on a minute after that.

"I've just sat down to dinner," he said.

"Sorry."

"Always happens. Sodde's Law of Telephones."

"So," I asked. "What's all this about Mallory?"

"Right." He paused to swallow something. "You know that we switched over to VDUs late last year?"

"I remember. There was practically a strike."

"That's it. Well, if you understand the principle of the things, you'll know they're not just used for writing copy for printers. They can also be used, and certainly are, for keeping detailed notes."

"It's always struck me as a risky method," I said. "But anyway, continue."

"A couple of the boys have spent the last few days extracting all of Sandy's entries, seeing if there's anything we can use. Most of it has been good, coherent stuff, but there's one entry for the day before his death that, frankly, we can't make head nor tail of."

I remembered the final jottings in his regular notebook. He'd been a deeply disturbed man.

"So what was the entry?" I asked. *"The Wall Street Journal* backwards?"

"Might as well have been. It was a single word, repeated over and over again."

I closed my eyes, and in my mind two faces melded into one. The first, a memory from fifteen years ago, lying in the bed in that field hospital and someone leaning over me; the second, from an hour ago, the face I had seen on the idol in the temple. Both the same.

"Don't tell me," I said quietly. "Let me guess. The mystery word is: *Nurse.*"

# CHAPTER 14

As nights go, this was an appalling one. I spent it trapped on the outer edge of sleep like a man on a cliff with his shoes nailed to the brink—couldn't fall, couldn't retreat, simply teetered endlessly. I sat in my favorite armchair and drank slowly and quietly and listened to the radio reports coming in.

Most of the Railton Road was on fire. A reporter came on and described the flames licking into the snow-filled sky as though he were reviewing some piece of really super-action art. The weather had turned the violence into something lunatic. A police van had skidded out of control into a mob, killing three, injuring twelve. The hand-to-hand fighting had become worse, more frantic, because it was practically impossible for anyone to run. Someone had let go at the police dogs with a shotgun.

"Mr. Du Pres?" asked someone in the studio. "As one of the most prominent community leaders in this area, do you have any explanation for the current, almost total breakdown of law and order?"

"I'm afraid the simple answer is, no, I do not."

"Ah—it was widely accepted that one of the major causes of the 'eighty-one troubles lay in what the community regarded as the belligerent attitude of the police, in particular the 'Swamp' operation. Would you say the same was true in this case?"

"As far as I'm concerned, the policing of this area—while not exemplary, don't get me wrong—has been reasonably nonprovocative, nonaggressive, over the past few months. If there was any specific tension arising between my people and the police, I certainly wasn't aware of it."

"Other factors cited have been poverty, unemployment, bad housing. Would you—"

"Now *look*, Mr.—what was it?—Nutley?"

"Knowley."

"Mr. Knowley. There's always been poverty, unemployment and bad housing. And of course they do nothing to help the social climate. But there'd have been a long build-up of tension if that was the case. You don't suddenly have ten thousand people leaping spontaneously onto the streets and burning everything in sight."

Long pause.

"Then, Mr. Du Pres, where do you suggest we find the solution?"

"Solution? I don't even know what the *question* is!"

No riots yet in the rest of London, but there had been isolated outbursts, a lot of them.

There were gang fights in the major parks.

Someone had gone berserk with a knife in Piccadilly Circus.

Someone else had fire-bombed the home of a famous politician.

The news from Paris and New York took second place now. But it was all bad. Very bad.

Around one in the morning I heard glass smashing down the street and I practically leaped out of my chair, the gap between the radio reports and my immediate reality closing fast. A solitary youth was walking down the obscured white line in the middle of the road throwing stones at all the downstairs windows. His movements were so disjointed someone else entirely might have been manipulating him, a marionette like the wooden ones I had seen back at the puppet theater. A police car pulled up three minutes later, and as the kid was hustled into the back seat he looked up and I saw his face. Corpselike in the flashing blue light. Blank as a sheet of unused paper.

I fell into a kind of doze about two hours later. I was back in the field hospital; the nurse was leaning over me, staring at me, smiling.

"Who are you?" I asked.

She did not speak.

"Please! Tell me what this is all about!"

Her smile did not alter one millimeter.

"I don't understand," I said. "What do you *want* from me?"

She opened her mouth.

And a torrent of blood came rushing out. I gave sleep up as a bad job after that.

Dawn came at last. The city tried to stretch and breathe, but it had just awoken from a nightmare, it was shaken, paranoid. By eight o'clock there were a few pedestrians on the streets; they scuttled past my window fast as windswept leaves. Everything was covered with an inch of snow; the little roadside trees in their wire cages; the fire hydrant farther down; the porches; the roofs. It should have been a fine, beautiful morning. I wanted to cry.

There was a pall of smoke across the south side of the river once again. This time, it would be a long while going away. I hovered anxiously around the flat until nine-thirty, then put in a call to the American Embassy, to a woman called Catherine Crosby.

"Hi," I said. "Remember me?"

"Don't I just." There was hammering in the background and she was talking loud above it. "You're the one who got surly with the ambassador last year."

I smiled. "I never take 'no comment' for an answer. Listen, I was wondering if you could do me a little favor?"

"How little?"

"Practically minute. I was in 'Nam for a couple of years covering the war and I got badly wounded in 'seventy. I got taken to a hospital at an airforce base. The surgeon there saved my life. I was thinking of doing a piece on him. You know, fifteen years on—what his reminiscences are, how the war affected him, what he's doing now, that kind of thing."

"It's a long time back."

"I'm sure he'll remember."

"Are you sure anyone's going to be interested?"

I was sure no one would, but it had been the best story I'd been able to come up with. "Let me be the judge of that," I said.

"I take it you want me to trace him for you."

"I'd really appreciate that."

She moaned. "You're an infernal nuisance, Mr. Auden. But, okay, I'll see what I can do. What was the surgeon's name?"

I had never forgotten it. "Augustus T. Elliot," I told her. "Captain."

She promised to get back in an hour. She was back in forty minutes.

"You're in luck," she said.

"How's that?"

"You might actually get to interview him face-to-face if you ask him very nicely. He's in England. He's stationed at the new airbase at Spellbrook. Do you have something to write on?"

She gave me the number of the base.

"And by the way," she added, "he's a colonel now."

"I'll remember to salute extra smart," I told her.

The hammering started up again just before I hung up. Everyone had their own personal headache this morning. I got through to the Spellbrook base and ended up repeating my story to the colonel's secretary, a Capt. Middlemarch. Yes. The colonel would be delighted to see me. Could we make it two o'clock?

I had my usual breakfast, shaved, got myself dressed presentably. I was just slipping on my raincoat to go out the door when the telephone started screaming. It was an idiot named Damien Fowler, so-called editor of something known as *Lookingglass: the Magazine of the Eighties*, to which I had promised an interview with John Boorman eight weeks

ago. He was nice to me at first. Then he
wheedled. Then he shouted. He told me he
had lots and lots of friends in the press
world. He told me he could make life very
bad for me. He told me that if I didn't have
the interview on his desk by tomorrow morning he would put around the word that Tom
Auden wasn't just a drunk anymore, he was
a burned-out, washed-up wetbrain who couldn't
be trusted with a used match stick, let alone
a commission.

He told me he was serious.

I told him to go fuck himself.

# PART THREE

# Strangers

# CHAPTER 15

The drive to Spellbrook took me two hours. The drive back, a lot longer. Partly because there was ice on the motorway, the traffic had slowed to an insectile crawl. But that was not the whole of it. I kept pulling onto the hard shoulder, trying to clear my head. I couldn't even think straight. My past no longer belonged to me. My memories had been turned upside down.

And the trail had led me back to the last person in the world I had ever wanted to see.

Just before the city limits, I stopped for the final time, walked up a snow-clad hill gone platinum in the moonlight. I stood there smoking, gazing over London. It looked like an immense jewel clutched in a glove the color of childhood shadows, the kind that lurked in every corner of the nursery when I was small, threatening so surely to engulf me I could not even scream. Among the yellow facets of lighted windows, sparks of red were already beginning to appear. New fires. Two across the river. One on the northern side. And if I imagined myself, right then, descending back into hell, I didn't know the half of it. . . .

Christine Mallory was getting packed to leave. She was wearing her smartest woolen suit, and when she opened the door for me, her eyes, below her newly tinted coiffure, were huge, her pupils like expanding blots of ink. A smile was frozen onto her lips, as though it had been there a long time before I had arrived.

No one in their right mind should have been smiling. The fire I had seen from that hill above London was blazing less than half a mile away, spreading. The noise of someone screaming echoed thinly toward us, then abruptly stopped. The roofs of the houses a few blocks away were lined at their edges with an orange glow.

"Hello, Tom," Christine said, focusing on me. "I'm in a mess. I suppose you're used to that."

There was a FOR SALE board next to the door, creaking tiredly in the wind. I brushed my fingertips against it as I walked in.

"Upping and running," I mused. "Where are you going to go?"

"I've family up North. Did I ever tell you that?"

"You might have. I don't remember."

She said, "So hard. You always were. But I can bounce right off you now." She went into the lounge, expecting me to follow her.

Two of her cases were already packed. The third was hanging loosely open, overfilled with sweaters and skirts all in neutral colors, as though she had chosen them not for display or comfort, but for camouflage. Once afraid, always afraid, whichever hole she bolted to.

Afraid of what? I asked myself. Sandy was dead now.

Once, in Elay, I worked with a girl whose husband knocked her about regularly, every three months. Nothing could persuade her to leave him. Suppose he kills you next time? I asked her. And she looked at me, and quietly said, *Then at least, I won't die alone.*

There was broken glass on the top stairs, from a smashed photograph. One of the bedroom windows must have been open—every so often a few shreds of torn notepaper would fall off the landing and spiral down like dead sycamore leaves. The last remains of Alexander Mallory's collected works.

In the lounge, Christine was making heavy work of trying to stand in one place. She was facing away from me, and her feet would move first left then right, seeking balance. Her head was tilted to one side, as though there was an old tune playing only she could hear.

She only became aware of my presence when I went to her handbag and emptied it onto the floor. I stooped to retrieve an opaque brown glass jar.

"How long have you been on these?" I asked.

The smile was still there. "As long as I can remember. Three days, perhaps."

"You got them on prescription?"

"Of course!" The light in her face was quite unnatural, like one of those *son et lumiere* displays that brought an abandoned building back to life for a few hours, except there was truthfully nothing there but dead stone, it was all an illusion. "I forgot," she said, "you despise weak people. Perhaps because you're weak yourself. You have a *weakness*, rather." She gestured to the drinks cabinet. "Help yourself. It'll be like old times."

And damned if I didn't feel abased pouring a drink, knocking it back, in front of her. She grinned all the while I did it. But I needed that drink.

I poured myself another.

"Did you tear up all of Alex's notes?"

"I always thought," she was saying, "you were one of those people who disproved the nastiness of alcoholism. Quite a romantic kind of drunk. Though not, of course, in the amatory sense."

"Christine?"

She went babbling on. "You all had your little weaknesses, you know. All four of you. The four flawed musketeers. You with your scotch. Sandy with his—should I call them ladies? No, I think not. We went to New York, stayed with the Rawlinsons once. We had to pay for our own food and most of theirs. Stuart lost the rest. Cards. And Peter Kyznik, so I understand, was a raving queer and a junkie. As though, what happened to you in Vietnam changed you all, left its own distinct little indelible mark. A flaw in the armor of the supermen. And look at you now, Tom. All flaw."

She stopped when I grabbed hold of her wrist. Her pupils shrank for a second, the smile on her face was ghastly.

"You're hurting me."

"You didn't answer the question."

"Is this your usual m.o.? No, don't stop. I'm quite enjoying it." But her eyes were becoming damp. "I thought you came to see *me*. Not to grub through some grubby bits of paper."

I tightened my grip.

"Only the stuff upstairs," she said at last. "I hadn't gotten round to the study yet."

I led her back through the hall.

"What's this all about?" she asked, only dimly curious.

"Sandy didn't commit suicide."

"Ohhh!" And she giggled.

"He was murdered, Christine."

"Good. Good. I wish I'd done it myself. Good, good, good."

I was practically carrying her by now. God knew how many of those pills she'd taken.

I went through the kitchen, opened the door onto Sandy's study. Clicked the light on.

He had built it in the rear half of the house's long garage, and it was always a mess, as though, now, all those piles of yellowing newsprint, those cuttings, those filled ashtrays, were as much a memorial to him as the graffiti, garbage, and parchments were to the inhabitants of Pompeii. But mess had never bothered me before. What always chilled me, stepping into that room, were the pictures on the walls.

It was like stepping into the fifteen-year-old past.

The walls were covered with black and white newspaper photographs from Vietnam.

A girl with her hair on fire stared back at me. She must have been about ten. A family wept by its dead ox. Pictures like ripped out memory cells.

He had bought six chests of drawers years ago at a jumble sale. They served as his filing cabinets. I went to the first drawer and began rummaging through it.

Christine came up from behind me and put her hands on my shoulders.

I kept my temper and said, very reasonably, "Why don't you go and sit down, Christine. Please? I won't be long."

Maybe it worked, I realized, because it was the first time in my life I had ever said *please* to her. I ignored the knotting in my stomach, carried on.

It took me practically half an hour to find the private journals. They were three large hardbacked notebooks, covered in a red cloth that had faded pink under the Oriental sun. Sandy had kept them every evening, right through our two years in Vietnam, and as soon as he'd been able to write after the horror in the jeep, he had sat there scribbling furiously in his hospital bed, bringing the journals up to date. He had never shown them to anyone. Not even Christine.

I flipped through until I found the entry for October 12.

Read it through about six or seven times. Then I leaned against the chest of drawers.

"I'll be damned" was all I could manage to whisper.

"Probably." Until I'd spoken, Christine had been somewhere very far away. I would not even like to guess where—perhaps in her childhood, sloughed of the body gone to seed, brain gone to putty, the bad, bile-tasting dough of recent memory. But the eyes were damp, and the smile, by now, had become almost sane. "What have you found, Tom?"

"Did Sandy ever talk to you about the day the jeep blew up?"

"All the time. *All* the time."

"You know, this is strange, he and I never discussed it. It was a kind of common bond we didn't want. Perhaps it would have pulled us too close together, made us really care, and I don't think either of us wanted that. If we *had* talked—Christine, he's got that day logged in his journal, every detail. It's not the same as I remember it."

She shook her drugged head. "It was a long time ago. You can't possibly—"

"We were both journalists, remember? If he and I had one thing in common, it was memory." I handed the journal to her. "He had us down as singing just before we reached the village—we weren't singing, we were listening to a cassette. He has Stuart getting out of the jeep at Sam Loong and taking photos of the *dinh*, the holy shrine. As far as I'm concerned, we didn't even stop there."

She was turning over the pages very slowly, gazing, as though she were studying the patterns rather than the individual words.

"The nurse," she mused. "He always used to mention her."

"There was no Vietnamese nurse, Christine."

And suddenly she was fully alert, looking up at me sharply. "That's ridiculous!"

"I went to see the guy who saved our lives today. Colonel Augustus Elliot. He was like Sandy, he kept records, too. Showed them to me. There was no *nurse*."

I moved away from the chest of drawers, went to the window. Twitching back the curtain, I could see sparks leap against the night sky half a mile away, the clouds above them turning the color of an alien sun.

"All the nurses under Elliot's command were American. It was written down right there, I checked all the names. Then I suggested, perhaps it wasn't a nurse. One of the menial staff perhaps. And . . . the hospital had had a gook scare a couple of days before the four of us arrived. Three Vietcong spies had gotten into the base. It was standard stuff, they'd pose as cleaners, laundrymen, shit-burners for a few weeks, blending in. And then the accidents would begin. Air bubbles injected into veins, plasma drips malfunctioning, the wrong drugs in the wrong bottles, that kind of thing. They caught all three, but they couldn't take the chance of there being any more. So no Vietnamese staff were allowed near the critical patients. And that very definitely included us."

"Sandy told me about it," Christine said. "But I suppose I never realized how terrible it must have been, never really knowing just who was the enemy."

"That was the least of it. Let me try something else on you. Sandy must have mentioned—it's down here in the journal— how we were out at the front of the convoy."

"On the way to—where was it?"

"Nha Trang. Except, according to the colonel, we were picked up six hours after the convoy had passed. We ended up *behind* it."

"Which is impossible!"

"Unless we stopped."

"Wouldn't the convoy have—?"

"Pressmen. We had the run of that country. We could do anything we liked. No one would have even noticed."

"And you don't remember anything?"

I pressed my forehead against the coldness of the window. "I've lost six hours out of my life. It feels like someone took me apart and scrambled the pieces when they were putting me back together."

"You were seriously hurt," she said. "You can't expect to remember everything."

"Except I have to. I've got no choice."

In the distance, a great shower of sparks hit against the darkness like tiny firework rockets, almost beautiful. I watched them glow. Christine came over from the chair and laid just one hand on my shoulder, and this time I was too tired and sick to resist.

We stayed like that for a while.

Then she said, gently, "You're living it all over again, aren't you, Tom?"

I buried my forehead deeper against the cold, cold glass. "Look at the streets out there. Look at the flames. It's as if the whole damned war's followed me back after fifteen years."

"If there's anything . . ."

"You can do? No, thank you, really. Unless you can tell me anything Sandy mentioned, anything which seemed out of place."

"I'm sorry. Nothing."

"Did he ever mention anything about a hiding place? Or about something very ugly and very bright?"

"No. Why?"

I grimaced. "I don't know. According to Elliot, it was something I was mumbling about in the field hospital. I was delirious. Perhaps I've always needed a hiding place."

The pressure of her hand had not changed once in all that while. I pulled away from the window, letting the curtain drop, and turned to look at her.

She was still unsteady from the drug. Her expression reminded me of someone who had discovered too much champagne for the first time. And yet, a person I had never really seen before was staring at me from the depths of that expression. Dante's hell had nine rings. Christine Mallory's—perhaps ten times that many, and all of them self-created.

Barriers. The bottle of pills, the drab clothes, the aged appearance she could have avoided, the purgatory marriage she could have walked out of years ago, the tears for herself, for no one . . . Heaven knew how many more. And barriers, Christine, work both ways. Perhaps you've always known that.

"You don't need to hide, Tom," she said. "You're strong inside. You always have been."

"Only strong enough for myself," I replied. "I can't pull anyone else with me."

She smiled quietly, understanding. "Anyone else . . . would be wrong to expect that of you. Were you," she asked, "ever close to getting married?"

"Once. Very close. That was a long time ago."

"I'm glad, anyway. I'm glad you knew that feeling."

"You and Sandy . . . ?"

"He was twenty-three. You should have seen him then, Tom. Pure energy. Pure white light. Do you think it was my fault it faded?" When I shook my head no, a tremor ran right up her body, a sigh that could not find escape. "I caught a glimpse of her, you know. His last venture. I knew there was something going on, and it was different to all the other little dalliances, more intense, so I borrowed a friend's Mini and I followed him all the way to Chelsea. I waited outside in the dark . . . oh, I don't know, about four hours, and then Sandy came down with her, and I caught the briefest glimpse, in the light from the open door. After that, they got into a car, one of those limousines, and disappeared into the night. So fast I didn't even try to keep up with them. It seemed appropriate, somehow."

"Was she an Oriental woman, Christine?"

"I wouldn't have called her a *woman*."

"How's that?"

"You think it was your nonexistent nurse? I doubt it, Tom. This was a girl. She couldn't have been much more than seventeen."

And either I had hit another dead end. Or it was just the beginning.

I said, "I've got to go now, Christine."

"Really have to?"

"Really."

We walked to the front door in silence. The noise of the riot seemed as far away as my own shattered past. Neither of us moved to open the door. I smiled at Christine.

"Will you make me one promise?"

"What is it?" she asked.

"Don't try to drive, not till those things wear off. I'd be worried as hell about you."

And she ducked her head, and laughed gently to herself. "Worried, after all these years. That's . . . nice." Her eyes were bright with tears. "Take very good care of yourself, Tom. I mean it."

"I will."

I kissed her, very softly, on the forehead. Then I went out into the night. The wind had changed direction. The flames were fanning up into the sky now, and all along the street, each shadow trembled in their glow.

I got into the car, locked myself in, practically floored the accelerator moving off.

The black Marine I had met at Plieku had been on night patrols for almost a year. Most other soldiers ended dead or insane long before that time, but this man was different. No stickers, headbands, helmet graffiti. His hair was at precise regulation length. All that evening, I watched him clean his rifle, sharpen his knife. His uniform was perfect, not a crease out of place. His boots, you could have skated on them. He pulled the lip of his helmet down level with his eyebrows. Fastened the strap under his chin.

He flashed me a huge white smile.

"Got *work* to do," he said.

# CHAPTER 16

I phoned the police as soon as I got home, got put through to Detective Inspector Grey. There was an unpleasant gloat to his voice I noticed straightaway.

"Yankee Doodle. Just the man I wanted to speak to."

"Isn't that a nice coincidence."

"We've got a warrant out on your friend Singh."

"Oh?"

"We found his prints all over the site of the Bhardwaj killing."

"That doesn't mean—"

"He's disappeared. We'll find him, though. The man's a bloody amateur."

"How about Mary and the kid?"

"She doesn't know a bloody thing. I went

at her for three hours, she just kept staring at me like she was made of wax."

I fought down the anger welling up in me. Later. Later. Right now, I needed Grey.

"Why were you looking for him yesterday?" he was saying.

"Another coincidence. A social call."

"Bullshit, Auden."

"Take it or leave it. I didn't find him anyway."

"Fancy perjuring yourself?"

"On my mother's life."

"You didn't *have* a mother. They grew you in a bottle."

"Look, Grey, I could spend all night exchanging pleasantries with you, but aren't you going to ask me why I phoned? I've got something you can use."

"Give."

"The Sam Loong Puppet Theatre."

"Very funny."

"Hilarious. You ought to meet these people, just your types."

Grey suddenly went quiet, perhaps because no one could make this up as a story. Perhaps because he was floundering, needed any lead, even the slimmest.

"Go on," he said.

"They've been following me around the last few days, ever since Sandy Mallory died."

"You think there's a link?"

"I really don't know."

"So?"

"Monday evening, I decided to approach them. Went to see their show. Tried to speak to them afterward. They beat me up."

"Aggravated assault. Where does that get me?"

"It gets them into one of your nice soundproofed cells. After that, who knows what they might confess to."

I could hear him pushing back his seat. "Okay, Auden. I want you down here in fifteen minutes to press charges."

"Wrong."

"You—"

"You pull them in, then I'll press charges. I'm not doing it any other way."

He was still screaming at me when I rang off.

John Stillman took a little longer to answer the phone. He sounded numb.

"How's the best organized-crime reporter this side of the pond?" I asked him.

"Overworked."

"No rest for the wicked."

"I wish the wicked would give me a rest. What can I do for you, Tom?"

"How many Vietnamese gangs do you know of operating in London?"

His voice went very cautious. "Large or small?"

"Large as they come."

He exhaled heavily. "It's hard to separate them out from the Tongs. There's so much Chinese influence, especially in anything financial. But you'd know that, of course."

"A rough guess?"

"Three, specifically linked with Vietnam. They operate all over the country. There's far more going on in the Midlands, for instance, than there is here in London. Protection, sweatshops, illegal immigration mostly."

I said, "This is a long shot, John, but were any of the three established over here before the boat people?"

"Two of them *were* boat people. Black marketeers. Why do you think they got out of Vietnam so fast? But the one you're thinking of is Lieu Fon Hut."

"Can you give me a run-down?"

"Where do you want me to start? He's the toughest of the three. Not very intelligent, but he commands a lot of respect. He has advisors to help him out with the brainwork. Around the end of 'sixty-nine they turned to him and said, 'Look, we've made a fortune here, we stick around and people are going to try and muscle in. A lot of time and trouble, not very profitable. So why don't we just lift our assets, transfer somewhere where there are easier pickings and no one's going to put a machete through your head.' "

"So they came here."

"Spot on. The man's of Chinese extraction

himself. A devout Buddhist, although his victims might question that. He went into action as soon as he arrived. Started with immigrants, expanded into anything you can think of."

"How do I get in touch with him?"

"Are you *mad*? Look, Tom, I don't want to pull rank, but I'm ten years younger than you, I've been doing this most of my working life, and I wouldn't go near the Viets with a bargepole. Most of the police won't either. These people cut their teeth on the toughest black market in the world! You don't play with them."

"I'm not playing. Let's just say I'm working on a hunch."

"It'd better be a good one. The best I can do is give you a list of Lieu's major establishments. After that, I just don't want to know."

"Not even if there's a story?"

"Leave it to me in your will," Stillman said.

I spent the next five minutes scribbling down the names of strip joints, blue movie theaters, betting shops. I finished up with a list of about thirty-five.

"What is this all about?" Stillman asked.

"A trick I learned from an editor once. You've got a handful of seeds, you don't know what kind of seeds. How do you find out?"

"Tell me."

"You plant them in the ground. You water them. And then you watch them grow."

Planting seeds.

Thirty-five phone calls. Thirty-five identical conversations.

My name's Tom Auden. I'm a journalist. I'd like to speak to Mr. Lieu. *Never heard of Mr. Lieu.* Well, just in case you do hear of him, here's my number and address. . . .

Planting seeds.

I went to get a drink, give my dialing finger a rest. Then I put in a call to a man I had not seen in years. And would never see again, as it turned out. Pastor Alec Hawkins had died last year. I found myself speaking to his daughter, Ginny.

Yes, I said, I remembered her very well. I was sorry to hear about her father. Could I come around there, first thing tomorrow morning? Yes, it was *very* urgent.

I switched off the answering machine, unplugged the phone, went into the bedroom with my bottle and set the alarm for six-thirty. Tomorrow was going to be a busy day.

It was the same dream, but a few of the details had changed. The sergeant still waited in the jeep. The four of us filed into the *dinh*. The mist was thick as ever. But now the eyes were watching us from inside, as though we had stepped into a cave and the creatures in the walls were marking our progress. Hungrily.

"Great! Great!" Rawlinson said, snapping away furiously with his Leica.

"But where's the human angle?" Peter Kyznik asked. "You tell me that."

Sandy Mallory pointed. "I think it's over there."

And there was the idol again, there was the marble slab. Except this time there were people standing around it. They were staring, but not at us. They were staring down.

The body on the slab was barely alive. Skin gone pallid. Face creased up with pain. And the lips moving softly, whispering. I could not hear what she was saying.

# CHAPTER 17

Drive past the elegant Georgian whiteness of Knightsbridge and Kensington, and you'll find Hammersmith, drab brown as a hibernating moth, the kind of color you would get if a thousand people chain-smoked for a thousand years. The traffic was heavy, the snow lay dirty in the gutters like the residue of bad dreams. The sky seemed low enough to touch. There were still traces of smoke in it and a couple of fires smoldering way across the river. A dark blue police van sat on nearly every corner. There were no pedestrians at all.

About four in the morning, a series of noises had woken me. I'd been dreaming again, of a riot I had witnessed in Saigon. When I'd gone to the window and stared out at the far end of the street, I'd seen a car, a Volkswagen, limping to the corner. One of the tires was down, and the car was veering from side to side on the packed snow, getting up about as much speed as a pushcart, but the man inside was still trying to drive it. He stopped trying when the vehicle slewed crosswise and hit a lamppost. The crowd who had been chasing him did not even consider stopping. The impact of the car had knocked the streetlamp out, there was only one more glowing, on the far side of the road . . . and against its wash of dim cold light the mob was silhouetted like a pack of wolves against the moon. Until that point I had still been blurred with sleep. After that, I went rigid. I could not have moved had I wanted to, as though the whole of existence had contracted to one eternal intake breath. The crowd fell on the car. They began slamming its sides with clubs, piping, lengths of chain.

It had happened to me once or twice in Vietnam. I could remember the frantic scramble to close all the windows, lock all the doors. And then the crouching there. And the wishing that you had taken your chances outside the car. Nothing, *nothing*, could be worse than being trapped inside that tiny, confined, escapeless space.

The mob hammered away for a while. Then they rocked the Volkswagen till it tipped over on its side. A couple of them went round to the back, levered open the hood. Set fire to the engine.

I went into the bathroom, threw up, drank some scotch and threw that up. Not because of the final glimpse of the driver struggling up through the door, clothes already on fire, but because . . .

What I had just seen on the street was an exact re-enactment of my dream—of a riot halfway round the world, fifteen years in the past.

Past, and dream, and present—all fused into one. That was why I was out here in the frozen world this morning. I wanted to understand. Dear God, I simply wanted to *understand*.

I turned off the Broadway into one of the narrow, muddy-looking streets that leads down to the railway track. The house I stopped in front of was a monstrosity, far older than its neighbors. Bars on the windows, all the way up. Solid oak, iron-studded door. Like a madhouse.

The door came open as I walked up the path.

I almost stopped and stared. If ever there were a more unlikely inhabitant of that house, it was Virginia Hawkins.

Framed against the interior darkness, she seemed as white and tall as something out of legend. Ash-blond hair flowed down across the shoulders of her gown. Her eyes were wide and green, guileless. She extended a hand to me. It was cold. Her cheeks were flushed against the wind.

"Mr. Auden. It's a pleasure to see you again."

"The last time I saw you, you were eighteen. I'm surprised you remember me."

"My father talked a great deal about you. The only journalist, he said, who wrote of him with complete fairness, complete honesty."

"I really was sorry to—"

"Cancer. He went very quickly, and with very little pain. I'd rather not talk about it."

She shut the door, led the way down the hall toward a chink of flickering light at the far end. The house was silent around us. It chilled me to think of her living here completely alone.

She was talking about the riots, how hideous they were. I broke in with, "Is the whole of this place still exactly the same?"

"Just as my father left it." She glanced over her shoulder and favored me with a pale smile. "You could say this is a museum now. I am the curator."

We walked into the living room. There was no living room like it in the world.

Imagine walking into a prison cell ten times its normal size. That was the effect of the bars on the window. Then imagine an old, stunted tree, bare of leaves now, just outside that window, its branches moving in the deadening December wind so that they cast sliding, impalpable shadows across half the room. As though a creature from the nightmare region of the brain were trying to get in, and only the bars were preventing it. A creature like that would have found plenty to amuse itself. Books, whole leather-bound walls of them, on every cult and sect and religion in the world. Ceremonial masks. Daggers, many of them stained brown with blood. Bowls, also stained. Other things, whose purpose I didn't even want to guess.

You expected to die before you ever got out of that room.

For several years after *The Exorcist* was released, it was a craze, a laugh, a story. Insane fundamentalist ministers got center-fold coverage in the popular press. Self-appointed demon killers glared at you from the cover of every cheap magazine. Bell, book, and candle. I had found one of the few genuine exorcists, Pastor Alex Hawkins. Part priest, part mystic, part psychologist. Wholly expert on every religion under the sun.

And with the kind of enthusiasm which is terrifyingly blind, he had passed it all on to Ginny.

The strange, broken light from the window was rippling across her. The shadow of a forked branch moved jerkily back and forth on her face, sectioning it into three unequal parts, like huge deep cracks on the face of a statue. Her smile was beautiful, but I could not respond to it. In this room, in this mausoleum of a house, she seemed as distant from the real world as a whitely gleaming, isolated star. Perhaps, it occurred to me, she was slightly mad.

"You said it was urgent?" she asked, showing me to a seat.

"I'd like to pick your brains for half an hour—anything you can tell me about Eastern cults."

She laughed. It came out as an almost metallic tinkle. "My father spent half his lifetime on the subject. You want half an hour."

"Typical journalist," I said. "Shall we begin?"

"One," I said. "The *thuggee* were supposed to have been wiped out in the nineteenth century. That's what we're led to believe. Is that true?"

"No, it isn't. You can't destroy a cult like the thugs with brute force and soldiers, or even spies." Ginny was sitting opposite me in a wing-backed black leather chair. Those green eyes of hers, in that icicle-white face, hardly seemed to blink, as though she were some kind of machine, giving answers. "Remember, they always were an extremely secretive organization. All they had to do was burrow underground a little deeper. This is mostly rumor, you understand, but the cult is slowly reappearing in India. Nothing like the same scale as before, but they are around."

"Just in India?"

"How do you mean?"

"Any other Eastern country, for instance? Or here?"

"You mean the Bhardwaj killing? I read about it in the paper." She shrugged. "Anyone can tie a *thuggee* knot."

"I think it was meant as a warning."

Her left hand, just clear of the chair, began to clench and unclench. Gently at first, but with increasing strength.

"Did they make any attempt to conceal the body? Was there sugar burned, or scattered on the floor?"

"Not so far as I know. Part of the *thuggee* ritual?"

"A vital part. Whoever killed him wasn't true *thuggee*. Something close, maybe."

"Okay," I said. "Let's try another tack. A four-armed idol. A goddess, perhaps. She's holding a sword, a shield, a noose, and a severed head. She wears a belt of human hands, and a necklace of skulls."

"Is she dancing?"

"Uh-huh."

Ginny chuckled. "We're back to the thugs

again. You're describing the goddess Kali."
She pointed behind me. "That book, the
brown one. Second shelf. Fetch it down, open
it to page twenty-seven."

And there she was on a full-sized color
plate. Only the face was different. It was
stylized, with bulging red eyes. The most
shocking feature was the tongue, poking
straight out like a raspberry baton.

"Why's she doing that?" I showed the
picture to Ginny.

"She was the wife of Shiva the Destroyer.
One day, an army of giants attacked heaven.
The gods elected Kali to defend them. She
took up her sword, tore off her clothes, and
waded into battle. And finally, the slaughter
became so great that even Shiva could not
stand it anymore. He . . . is something
wrong?"

My head was whirling, the room had gone
away from me. I was back in the telephone
box three days ago with that insane Oriental
woman's voice coming down the line at me
like something fanged and hungry. *Let me tell
you about my mother*, she had said. *Let me tell
you.*

"Shiva," I completed, almost to myself,
"ran out onto the battlefield, lay down among
the dead, hoping to make Kali stop. But she
didn't. She killed him. And then she spat her
tongue out."

*And the mad woman hung up.*

I was back in the room again, staring down at the picture in the book. Kali was dancing on her husband's corpse. Behind her was the same frieze I had seen in the riverside temple. The stabbed man. The hanged man. The crushed man. The man beheaded.

Ginny was looking at me strangely.

"Tell me about Kali," I said.

"I'd like to know—"

"Just *tell* me," I almost yelled.

She settled back in her chair. The hand was still clenching and unclenching. "She is the Hindu goddess of death. One of their most awesome and potent deities. She has her equivalent in every ancient religion of the East. In Egypt she was known as Sekhet or Hathor. In Syria, Anath. She has a concealed third eye of supernatural power. And she's a mistress of disguise. She gives life, only to take it away again. The *thuggee* worshiped her devotedly. Many Indians, the Bengalis for instance, still do."

"Great. Charming."

"It's not the way you imagine," she said. "Religion, you see, is a reaction to circumstance. Take the most potent force in your part of the world, make a god of it. You don't find the Eskimos worshiping rain, for instance. You do find Third World nations worshiping death, because it's all around them, every day of the year. Have you ever heard of Sitala?"

I shook my head.

"She's the major goddess in the Indian backwoods. She controls smallpox. That may sound revolting to you, but among those primitive tribes smallpox is *the* major regulator. Similarly with a group of addicts preparing their heroin fix. It's a religious ritual."

Her expression altered a moment. Her eyes glazed with—pain? Then she smiled.

"Besides," she continued, "like most Westerners, you don't understand the Hindu ideal. It's the most diversified religion in the world. It accepts all philosophies and all beliefs, however contradictory they might seem. And the gods are not well-defined individuals. They assume different characters, different names. Even, in the case of the one in question, different colors. As Kali she is black, ferocious, deadly. As Uma she is white, pure, virginal. She has about a dozen names. Deva, Parvati, Sati, Durga, Jagadgauri—"

"Say that again?"

"Jagadgauri."

The name of the princess in the puppet show.

"The yellow woman," Ginny was saying. "They call her the Harvest Bride."

"She"—I shook my head, trying to clear it—"isn't worshiped anywhere outside India?"

"A few small Hindu communities. Very few."

"Not in a place called the kingdom of Champa? There's no such place, is there?"

"Not now, but there used to be. On the Eastern coast of Indochina. Nowadays," Ginny said, "we'd call it Vietnam."

I spent the next half hour reading about Champa.

It was never the Buddhist country Vietnam is. Even before its foundation as a kingdom near the end of the second century, Hindu priests and scholars had been there, spreading their own religion, their own culture. Sanskrit became the sacred language of the Chams; they turned into an Indianized, Hinduized people. And yet, they did so by choice. India never conquered them.

No one ever conquered them for long.

The names of great warlords sprang from the printed page. Indravarman. Bhiadravarman. Che Bong Nga. They slaughtered their own officials, dissidents, and relatives like flies, and then turned their attention to the outside world. None of their neighbors was safe, right up to Imperial China. No trading ship, from the Gulf of Tonkin to the China Sea, sailed without fear of the Chamic fleet. They could not grow much in their mountainous coastal land, had few natural resources, so they killed and stole.

And finally, one of their neighbors had enough.

The Vietnamese we know today originally lived in the southmost end of China. They were brilliant warriors in their own right—they defeated Kublai Khan's hordes three times in thirty years—but they needed land for their expanding, starving people, and they were sick to exhaustion of the cruel, deadly hyena that was Champa. Under the Le dynasty, principally under Le Thanh Tong, they made the great push south, furious and desperate. And this time, not even the Chams could stop them. Except . . .

Look at most history books and they will tell you Champa was destroyed in 1471. Not true. A tiny kingdom remained, in the concealed bays just below Nha Trang, right up until the 1600s. And every so often a merchant ship from Canton or Bangkok or Singapore would never reach its destination. And the wives and children in the silent waiting ports would know exactly why. There were only three thousand Chams left in Vietnam today, pale brown people with high brows, caucasian noses, and black twisted hair. Most of them lived in the Binh Dinh province. The area around Sam Loong.

"Is it possible," I asked Ginny, "that they've some cult, the equivalent of the *thuggee*?"

"What better place for a goddess like Kali," she said, "than a country like Vietnam?"

Her left hand had stopped clenching and unclenching now. The expression on her face was beatific. Drops of blood were falling from her open palm, red as tiny roses.

# CHAPTER 18

I was still thinking about her less than five minutes from home, when two things happened at once. The skies began to snow again, letting down the first few scurrying flakes like a hand releasing ashes. When I switched on the wipers and glanced in the rearview mirror, the limousine dropped in behind me. It was huge, black, with polarized windows keeping it threateningly blind. The way it swooped in from the fast lane reminded me of a hawk descending on a sparrow.

There was the urge to panic at first. Let go of the steering wheel and let events take their final course. The black limousine moved right up to my bumper, remained there, four inches from impact. I wished to God that I could see the driver's face. The damned thing might have been driving itself.

Stillman warned you, laddie. You asked for this yourself.

I decided to give them a hard time. It wouldn't fetch me a reprieve, but at least it might earn some respect. They had come for me as though I were some garbage to be scooped off of the street, and I wasn't going to give them that kind of satisfaction.

When I took a sharp left, it was the wrong direction into a one way street.

I practically went up onto the sidewalk to avoid the oncoming traffic. Cars swept by like brushmarks, horns screaming. When I reached the safety of the next turning, the black limousine was still firmly on my tail. I swung over, thumping up across the curb, and doubled back the way I had come.

The limousine was still there, at the same distance. There was no point even contemplating outrunning something of that size and power. Trying to earn some respect, I had made myself look like a complete fool. I drove slowly, wearily, back toward my apartment block.

Then, practically outside the front door, I allowed myself a gentle smile, and stamped sharply on the brake.

I was still smiling when they dragged me out of the car and past the limousine's ruined front grille. I even smiled when one of them punched me, hard, in the stomach.

"What's the matter? Aren't you insured?"

They bundled me into the rear compartment.

I suppose it was Mr. Lieu. It might have been one of his lieutenants, but the three who had picked me up behaved very nervously around him, keeping their distance, as though he were surrounded by an invisible wall and there were beautiful murals on it and God help anyone who damaged them. It was dark in the basement where they had taken me, and I could not see his face. Only his eyes. There was some kind of loud music playing on the floor above; no tune filtered down this far, but the basement trembled with its rhythm. It made my bones vibrate and set my teeth on edge.

I had been forced to kneel. My hands were already cuffed behind me. I was in the square of light from a single tiny window. The light was cold and gray. There was blood trickling down the side of my mouth—it had taken all three of them to get the cuffs on me.

"I told you not to hurt him," the man whose face I couldn't see said.

One of the three answered in Vietnamese.

"I told them not to hurt you."

"Fine," I said.

"Journalist, aren't you?"

"Yes."

"Stupid journalist."

"Yes."

"Real idiot."

"Really idiotic."

"Why were you looking for Mr. Lieu?"

"Have I found him?"

"Why were you looking for him?"

"Yes, I've found him."

"I don't like to ask questions three times."

"That's sad."

"Stupid journalist."

"Yes."

"Hurt him," the man said to one of the others. Then: "Why were you looking for Mr. Lieu?"

"If he does that again he'll lose his foot. I've rabies."

"Hepatitis, more like. Why?"

"Big word, hepatitis."

"Hurt him."

"That wasn't fair."

"Life isn't fair."

"No."

"Why?"

"Why was I looking for Mr. Lieu?"

"Now we're getting somewhere."

"Get me off my knees."

"No."

"Get these cuffs off me."

"No. Why were you looking for Mr. Lieu?"

"Have I found him?"

"No such person. Why are you making things difficult for yourself?"

"That's just the way I am."

"Too bad."

"Yes."

"Do I have to ask the question again?"

"You a Buddhist?"

"No such person as . . . *good* journalist."

"Your men Buddhists?"

"Clever journalist."

"Any of them Chams?"

"Hurt him."

When I came back from where I had gone, one of the men still had his shoe in the back of my neck and was turning the heel.

"Tell him to stop doing that."

"No."

"Tell him."

"Sorry."

I blacked out.

"Why were you looking for Mr. Lieu?" the voice asked as I swam back toward the light. I blacked out again.

Two of the men yanked me back to my knees and shook me.

"You heard the question."

"What question? Oh, that question."

"You did hear it."

"Yes."

"Answer it."

"Buddhist?"

"Answer it."

"All of you?"

"Answer."

"Ever bring in any Chams?"

"Answer."

"Around 1970, 1971?"

They stopped. It was very quiet for a while, except for the music. They filed out of the room and closed the door behind them.

They left me kneeling there for well over an hour. It was the same four who came back in the end. Their faces loomed around me.

*What do you know about Chams?* they asked me. I told them I knew about a whole village of them. *No. Not a whole village of them. What did I know about Chams?* I told you. *What do you know?* Listen, let go of my collar. *What do you know about 'seventy-one?* A lot of things. *What things?* A lot. I got shipped back home that year. *What do you know about boats?* They're the things that sail on water. *Boats and Chams. What do you know about them?* How many were there? *What do you know?* Where are they now? *Boats and Chams. What do you know?* You're hurting me. *Who told you this?* Nobody told me. *Tell us the name.* Nobody told me, I knew myself. *How did you know? How much do you know?* Nothing, I know nothing. *What do you know?* Nothing, I tell you!

"Is this to do with the riots?" came another voice from out of the corner. It was a quiet but deep voice, almost accentless.

The four others stilled into silence. I strained my eyes, but one of them was almost swollen shut and all I could make out was a very dim outline against the blackness of the corner. "I don't know," I said.

"Is this to do with the fact that the Vietnam of fifteen years ago has come to London?"

"Maybe. I don't know. Maybe."

"Is that why you came here?"

"Yes."

There was a quiet laugh in the voice. "Is that what you risked your life for?"

I nodded slowly. The black outline was not moving at all. I was not even sure it was there.

"Who *are* you?" the voice asked.

"I don't know." I felt very old, and tired, and injured.

"Who are you?"

"I'm Tom Auden. I'm a journalist."

"So you are."

"Are you Mr. Lieu?" I asked.

"No."

I nodded. "What are you going to do with me?"

The way I asked that question, anyone listening might have decided I didn't really care what the answer was—and that listener would have been wrong. I did care. I did care very much. I had been scared from the moment they had bundled me into the car. And the terror had wormed so deeply into me that I was not even able to show it, it had me by the inside of the throat and the moment it let go I would begin screaming and never stop.

Is this where it ends? In a black damp cellar kneeling in a patch of frozen light, that discreetly, that pathetically? *I deserve more respect than this.* I had seen those words, unspoken, on the faces of a thousand men close to death. I may not be much, I may have done some bad or stupid things, I may not be Michelangelo or Wolfgang Amadeus Mozart, and you may not like my politics or my morals or even myself, but I have run through fields bursting with flowers and felt the sunlight on my face and made friends and laughed and had special moments once in an occasional while, and I have made love with the moonlight coming through the curtains and had people love me, I have touched and cried and played with children and walked home alone with only the night and the rain as companions and I have woken in the morning and smelled the world after the rain and that may not count for a hell of a lot but I am a human being and *I deserve more respect than this.*

The blow to my neck came so quickly I barely felt it.

# CHAPTER 19

Gray. I knew that color long before I opened
my eyes and saw it. Pale, textureless, amorphous gray. I could taste it in my mouth, feel
it wash over my skin beneath the thinness of
my clothes. It was there beneath my fingertips as they flexed and clawed against the
winter soil. Above me and below me—two
thin strong sheets of gray were pushing in on
me like the jaws of a great crusher.

I opened my eyes and saw the tombstones.

There were bare trees over in the corner of
the graveyard. They were whispering in the
wind, and the thin frozen grass between the
stones was tossing back and forth and whispering, too. Each time the wind rose a
couple of notches, the sound turned to a
shriek that made my head pulse and my eyes

squeeze closed. There was a pain in the small of my back, and another farther up at my neck. I was not sure if I could get up.

There were two tombstones directly in front of me, side by side, like the twin slabs of the commandments.

A car hurried by somewhere behind me. Whoever was in it did not see me, or if they did, never bothered to stop. I had been lying there, unconscious, for so long that my skull felt frozen, it felt like iron that had been chilled so long that if you tapped it with a hammer it would suddenly explode. I was completely numb, sickeningly so, pains like great lizards in my chest. *I couldn't feel my legs.*

Perhaps it was that—a terror born and nourished fifteen years ago—which finally drove me to my feet.

There was an old, lightning-blasted stump of a tree near me, black and white with its thin powdering of snow, and I supported myself on it, clung to its fossilized limbs, and shook and ached so violently I thought I would die there. Cold is a drug in its own special league, a white lady who guides you so slowly toward death that you end up not caring where the journey leads so long as you can find sleep at the other end. Pain gone. Dignity gone. Barely human anymore. In an open patch of gravel off to my left, I could see the tire marks where the limousine had stopped. Concentrate on that, Auden. Concentrate on it. I was in a tiny cemetery somewhere in west London, with tall, crumbling Victorian houses across a stretch of wasteland in one direction and a major road, traffic humming restlessly by, in the other. I could make out two furrows in the mud where the Vietnamese had dragged me from the limousine, dumped me in front of the tombstones.

The inscriptions were hidden by snow. I took a step toward them, stumbled to my knees. From that position, I reached out and wiped the snow clear, cutting my hands, barely feeling it.

They were husband and wife.

CHA THAN TON, the stone said.

And CHA HUEN LIN.

DIED 1971.

It took me practically half an hour to get a taxicab. I had to walk from the tiny, disused municipal graveyard right to the Shepherd's Bush roundabout, and even then the first half-dozen cabs flashed by, the drivers glancing at me and then staring straight ahead. I caught a glimpse of my reflection in a shop window and could not blame them.

By the time I got out at the Porchester Baths my teeth were rattling and the movement of the taxicab was making me dry-heave. I went inside, stripped in a cubicle, and sat for over an hour in the Turkish baths until the waves of shivering and sickness passed. My clothes were dry when I got back to the cubicle. I dressed carefully, then went along the street until I found a bar. Two scotches left me exhausted and drugged, but my body felt my own again. The first approaching cab stopped when I hailed it this time. Where's the town hall for this area? I asked the driver, pointing to the cemetery on his map.

Ten minutes later I was walking up the front steps of a gray, faceless pillbox of a building with dim yellow lights showing through its windows like candles for the dead. It had pale blue tiles and acoustic ceilings inside. A typewriter rattled from one of the offices. I walked down the empty lobby until I found the door marked BIRTHS, DEATHS, AND MARRIAGES. A bell rang as I went in. The man behind the counter looked up, saw the bruises on my face and spent the rest of his time trying not to stare at them.

"My name's Tom Auden." I flashed him my press card and waited while he took it in. "I'm doing a story on illegal immigration. What happens to the immigrants, where do they end up, do they ever end up dead. I need some help on two in particular."

He looked at me oddly, asked why he hadn't heard from his superiors about this. He was a florid-faced little man, forties to early fifties, with a gray mustache and wispy, curling hair that hung untidily around the bald patch at the center; he looked as though he could do with some new clothes and twenty-four hours' sleep.

"It's just two people," I said. "Two dead people. Give me a break here."

He shot the tiniest of glances at my face again, so that I reached up and touched my swollen lip self-consciously. For a moment, he seemed to be considering. Then he smiled and nodded.

"Illegal immigrants?"

"That's right."

He lighted a cigarette, offered me one. "Some very difficult cases there. If we can trace their families, their homelands, then we'll generally send the bodies back. You wouldn't believe how difficult that is in the total absence of documentation. All we might have is a name, perhaps even a false one."

"No," I said, "these two were buried here, quite a while back. Two Vietnamese."

"Unusual." His eyebrows came up.

"Their names were Cha Than Ton and Cha Huen Lin. If you could look them up—"

He took another drag of his cigarette, still smiling. "I don't need to, Mr. Auden. That would have been . . . 1971?"

"That's right."

"They were some kind of Vietnamese sub-culture. Indianized, I think. Husband and wife. No question of sending them back, the war was still on."

"You seem to remember it pretty well, for fourteen years ago."

"Not easy to forget," the little man said. "They killed each other. Suicide pact."

He got me their last recorded address out of the files, and I dutifully wrote it down. I thanked him and went back onto the street.

It was one of those days in an English winter when evening begins at two in the afternoon, the clouds drawing together and darkening until all that remains of the sunlight is a band of oranges and silver-grays at the far, remote horizon. Most of the cars had their headlights on, and most of the houses I passed had lighted windows. I glanced in through a couple of them at the tiny, warm-looking room within. In one, a young blond woman was sprawled in an armchair watching her television set, quite motionless. In another, two older women were sitting at a pine table, drinking coffee, talking animatedly, the barrier of glass and space between us turning their moving lips and rapid, integrated gestures to mime.

*A suicide pact.* I turned it over and over in my mind. Those two Chams, whoever they had been, had surreptitiously left a country where they might be shot for leaving, traveled seven thousand miles, been smuggled by the Lieu network into a country cold and alien in every way. Only to die. Why would they travel so very far, only to die?

A band of schoolchildren hurried past me as I turned the corner. Benningden Street twisted into the gloom ahead of me like a narrow, tree-lined gulley in some hill of crumbling red rock. All the black bare trees had overgrown their cages till the branches almost touched. The only lights on were behind drawn curtains.

Number 99 was around the second bend, the central of three run-down terraced houses that had been boarded up and sealed with sheets of corrugated iron as though that might conceal them from view. I backtracked to a newsagent's I had noticed a couple of turnings away, bought a flashlight and a set of batteries. It bumped gently in my pocket as I fished out an iron bar from the surrounding rubble and levered open the back door of number 99. I went in carefully, testing the floorboards with each step. The cold had begun fighting back up inside me. My head throbbed a little, and I tried to ignore it.

The rain had been getting in for several years. It had collected in the room above and torn down an entire corner of the kitchen ceiling; the wall below it looked like rotting black plastic; the kitchen units were thick with white mold. A Mickey Mouse eggcup, most of its paint chipped away, stood waist-deep at the edge of the mold as though in a white, spreading sea. I clamped a handkerchief over my mouth and nose and went on through.

In the hallway and the lounge, the color had gone but patterns still remained on the wet, peeling wallpaper. It had been a pleasant house once. Almost buried beneath the odor of rot were human smells from the generations who had lived here. Only the motionless shadows inhabited it now—one day, my own home would look this way. I shone the flashlight beam into a corner. Silverfish wriggled away beneath the skirtings.

The staircase was so cocooned with spider webs it seemed to be supported by the intricate gray veils. They reflected my beam of light, layer after layer, and sent it back as a shimmering, gently waving blur. There were penny-sized black spiders at the center of most of the webs, with smaller black dots—the remains of their lunches—sprinkled randomly around them. I brushed aside the first few layers. When I placed my foot carefully on the bottom step, it turned out to be as insubstantial as pulp.

I began to search the ground floor inch by inch. Lifting the edges of the carpet was the worst—they would stick to the floorboards for a long while, and then suddenly come free with a ripping noise and the smell of decomposing rags. There was not even the habitual sheets of old newspaper underneath, not a dropped coin, not a pin, nothing in the entire house. I felt up inside the chimney shaft and there was a rusty nail there, nothing more. It had begun to gently rain outside. First, I could hear it tapping on the roof. Then, it started dripping through brown cracks in the ceiling, trickling down the walls. Slowly at first, but then with increasing speed until the beam of my torch was broken up with silver flashes like big down-dropping insects, drumming on the carpet as they hit.

I started to pull up the floorboards. They came away easily in my hands, sometimes tearing in the middle like stiff old rubber. After the first few splinters, I wrapped my handkerchief carefully around my right palm. I made a large enough opening and then got down inside, crouching, shining the torch right to the bare brick edges of the walls. Again, nothing. I went to the skirting boards, yanking them away. But when I eventually did find something, it was in the kitchen, covered by the white devouring mold.

The envelope had decomposed to black and came to tiny muddy pieces in my fingers. Inside were four stiff rectangles covered in the same damp black. I wiped them clean. They were printed cards in plastic holders, each with a pin fastened onto the back.

The cards had yellowed now, the print had

faded. But I had no trouble recognizing what they were. We all used to wear them as well as the dog tags around our necks. We had them pinned over the left breast pocket of our battle dress, and they were like a key that sometimes opened doors and sometimes closed them, changed moods and conversations and attitudes all around us, made us anything but invisible, anything but invulnerable. Four military issue press cards from the Vietnam war, like relics in some cultural museum. Each with a name on it.

*Peter Kyznik.*

*Stuart Rawlinson.*

*Alexander Mallory.*

I held the last card in the torchlight for a long while.

*Thomas Auden.*

# CHAPTER 20

The cab driver pulled up outside my apartment building and I paid him and got out; the cab made a loud puttering noise against the rain as it drove away. My car was still parked half in and half out of the gutter, the rear end smashed and the lights broken. I started it up and parked it. Only when I got out, and glanced up toward the fourth floor, did I see that the lights in my lounge were on. I went up the back way, by the fire escape, and let myself in through the kitchen.

Someone had taken all the crockery out of the sink and dumped it on the floor. Someone had also opened every cabinet and swept the contents out, most of which had broken. The kitchen clock hung unscrewed from the wall. The lampshade was lying in the corner along with some broken plates.

The same person or people had taken a knife to the mattress of my bed and emptied the dresser drawers out onto the floor. They had overturned my living room furniture and torn the pictures down and dismantled the back of the television set. An open bottle of scotch lay overturned on the carpet, empty now, the room stinking of alcohol from the stain. And they had been into my desk. God knew why I had ever kept that picture. The person in it, slim, twenty-two, standing on a Californian beach with his back to the ocean, bore no resemblance to the Tom Auden I had become. They had broken the glass and torn the picture out, crumpled it and thrown it on the floor. I tried to smooth it out as best I could, then laid it carefully on the desk and tried to forget about it.

The bedroom telephone was not working. Neither was the one in my lounge. The cord had been yanked loose at the rear. I had learned how to repair such things years ago, deadlines and repairmen usually not coinciding. Then I went around the apartment switching off most of the lights. Far across the river, the new night's fires were already beginning, weak orange against the rain, but growing obstinately stronger till their patterns danced against the far wall of the lounge, flickered among the overturned furniture and the debris. I lifted my hand and it too had pale orange shadows lapping across it; it was hard to tell where the shadow left off and the hand began.

My mind went back to those identity cards in the house.

I sat down in the middle of the floor with the telephone on my lap, dialed the international operator, got the number of *La Bête Rouge*, a left-wing small circulation newspaper Peter Kyznik had been working on ever since he had left Montreal for Paris eight years ago. I hadn't spoken to him in half a decade. My mouth and throat felt dry.

I spent the next ten minutes struggling with my bad French until I got put through to the editor. I carefully explained that I wanted to speak to Peter Kyznik.

The editor's voice became quiet and guarded. There was a long pause, filled only by the static on the line, like the whisper of electric rain.

Who exactly wants to speak to him? he finally asked.

I felt my stomach shrink. Oh, no. Oh, God. Peter? The room seemed to contract around me.

I explained to him exactly who I was. He was very sorry to inform me that Peter Kyznik had died three weeks ago.

How? I asked him.

*Il s'est pendu*. It is the French for "he

hanged himself." I'm sorry, *m'sieur.* This came as a terrible shock to us all. Peter was a good man and a very fine journalist.

Yes, he was, I said quietly. When I finally hung up a minute later, all that I could hear, all I wanted to hear, was the sound of the rain on my lounge window.

I was shaking.

Perhaps it was not shock that was taking hold of me. Perhaps, deep inside, I had known what the answer would be before I even made that call. *Paris. Paris. The Sam Loong Puppet Theatre had been there three weeks ago.* But it was insane, the whole thing. What was I investigating here? My own impending death? "The ultimate story," my old editor in Los Angeles would have said, and smiled.

Slowly, very slowly, I picked up the phone again and began to dial the number of Stuart Rawlinson in Manhattan.

"Rawlinson residence," announced a teen-age girl at the other end. I could hear she was chewing gum.

She must have been about sixteen now. I struggled to remember her name. "Is that Josie? Look, I'm not even sure you remember me. I'm Tom Auden."

Her voice took on a slightly wary, hostile edge. "Oh, sure. You were one of Daddy's pals, weren't you."

"I heard a rumor that your mom and Stuart split up. Is that right?"

"Yep."

"I'm sorry to hear that."

"No one else is."

There was no heat in her voice. All the violence in it was bland and cold and unyielding as a carving knife.

"Hey, look," I said, swallowing, "can I speak to your mother?"

"Mom's out," Josie said.

"Well, I'm sorry to disturb you, but could you tell me how I can get in touch with your dad?"

"Try a Ouija board. He's dead. Good-bye."

"Hey, wait, no, Josie! Are you still there?"

There was the noise of chewing at the other end.

"Josie," I said, softly, "how long ago did your father die?"

She finally said, "Two months."

"Oh, God. Look, Josie, I hate to do this to you, but I need to know exactly how he died."

"He fell under a subway train," she said, totally impassively, "and was crushed to little, tiny pieces. I'm in the middle of watching a movie. Can I go now?"

She waited a few seconds, and then, when she got no reply, hung up. And that was the end of Stuart Rawlinson. Me, I was remembering a day fifteen years ago. The day before our jeep went over the mine. We were both mildly stoned and were discussing—in our phased, patternless way, conscious more of the sunlight on our skins than of each other's words—we were discussing immortality through the printed word, the reproduced picture. Stuart became suddenly intense. He leaned toward me, face all angles and shadows even then, hair turning prematurely gray. There were shells going *whump, whump* in the distance, about twenty miles away.

"I used to believe that," he told me, "they read you after you're dead, see your pictures, so a part of you lives on. It's nothing. It doesn't even begin to compare with . . . look." He reached into his wallet, took out a color Kodachrome of a blond-haired baby girl. "That's Josie. That's *my* immortality."

And he had been so happy. So proud.

The disconnect tone echoed around the flat. I put down the phone, switched off the final lights, made my way toward the bedroom. I pulled the ripped mattress into place and spread a blanket over it, trying to make it as comfortable as possible; I kicked off my shoes and removed my tie and lay down, wrapping the continental quilt around me. All the aches in my body had come alive, throbbing dully. I shifted around and tried to sleep, the flickering orange glow coming in through the doorway. Somewhere, several days behind me, a puppet's head was still bouncing from the stage, still rolling. My face on it. My face!

Three different deaths. Each ghastly and macabre. I could remember, as clearly as though I were standing there, the frieze behind the idol of Kali in that warehouse by the river. The strangled man. The impaled man. The crushed man. The man beheaded.

Peter Kyznik. Hanged.

Sandy Mallory. Impaled.

Stuart Rawlinson. Crushed beneath a subway train.

*Tom Auden* . . . ? The puppet's head bounced. Tom Auden . . . ?

Just as I drifted into sleep, I thought I saw a shadow move toward me, bringing something sharp and silver down toward my neck.

# PART FOUR

# The Harvest
# Bride

# CHAPTER 21

It was still raining when I woke, in a steady black downpour; my bedroom was dark gray, colorless, with all the shadows nestling in it like night creatures, flapping, membrane-winged bats. A bolt of lightning splintered down behind the curtains. Thunder prowled across the sky between the low, devouring clouds. It was eight o'clock.

I groaned and sat up, still wrapped in the continental quilt, and gazed around me at the motionless wreckage of the room.

"The morning after the night before," I mumbled to myself. "And I didn't even have a very good time."

There was the taste of bile in my mouth, but apart from that all the cold and sickness was gone. My stubble itched. So did the gum in my eyes, and my whole body seemed to crawl beneath my sweaty, battered clothing. I headed for the lounge, and then the kitchen, undressing as I went. There was an envelope waiting for me on the doormat in the hall.

It had airmail stickers and American stamps on it. It was marked LOS ANGELES, and had been posted four days ago. I smiled as I opened it. In all the years I had worked with Petrie Kowalsic at the *Los Angeles Herald*, he never *had* given up the habit of pounding the typewriter keys so hard he practically punched character-shaped holes through every page.

Dear Tom,
  Sorry to have taken so long getting this to you, but I wasn't sure whether I was making a big deal out of nothing. About five, six weeks ago, word went around that a group of, so the rumor goes, Vietnamese were in town looking for you, just asking around, very quiet and suspicious. They left for Europe a while later. Thought you ought to know.
                                    Yours paranoidly,
                                              Petrie

*Thanks, Petrie*. I crumpled the page up and threw it in the kitchen bin, then busied myself in the bathroom adjusting the shower to a bearable temperature. Later, I rummaged through the chaos in the lounge till I found a small, unbroken bottle of vodka, and that made a pleasant change. I had forgotten it was there. I took a mouthful and it bit into me like stainless-steel fishhooks, and I choked and wiped my running eyes. I began the job of putting the apartment back into some kind of order, safe and warm in the glow of the electric light while the rain hissed and the thunder roared outside.

The bedroom telephone was the last job. It clattered when I picked it up. Fixing it took a while. I had just put the screwdriver down and was sitting on the edge of the bed when the damn thing rang.

Detective Inspector Grey said, "Auden, we've just brought the Sam Loong Puppet Theatre in. I want you down here right away."

"Auden," he said, "are you listening?"

I blinked. "Oh, sure," I said slowly. "All ears."

"*Well*, Yankee Doodle?"

I thought about that sharp-edged blade waiting to find my neck, somewhere out there in the rain. I thought about the fear and the terror and the pain of yesterday, and how warm and secure my apartment felt. Then I found myself thinking about Christine Mallory in tears and Peter Kyznik hanging there and Stuart Rawlinson holding out that stupid photograph so many years ago.

I sighed into the mouthpiece. "Where did

you find them?'' I asked, quietly reaching for a pen.

''Does that matter?''

''It might. Be nice to me, Detective Inspector.''

''Soho. Back alley behind Macclesfield Street, over the top of a Chinese emporium.''

I wrote it down.

''Stop playing about and get your arse down here, Auden,'' Grey said. ''I want that statement from you.''

''No statement, Grey.''

He took in breath for a second. I could imagine him turning red behind the phone.

''Remember who you're talking to now, Auden.''

''No statement,'' I repeated. ''I'm dropping the allegations.''

''If you think—''

''I was probably drunk when I made those allegations. You really ought to be more careful, Inspector, where you get your information from.''

''*Auden*—''

''No statement? No charges? There are such things as Judges' Rules, Inspector. You'd really better let them go.''

I was still pondering that I had never heard *that* word in exactly *that* context before when I hung up the phone. I dragged on some socks and shoes and a jacket, found my coat, and went out into the rain. It was coming down like knives—that rain—all over London.

"When do you think it's going to stop?" the Green Beret had said, in the bunker at Plieku.

I turned around and stared at him in the half light of the bunker. He was short and going thin, and had one of those faces that reminded me of a sickly five-year-old, a child unable to sleep because the closet door keeps swinging open. I had been writing up some notes until he spoke. Now, I laid the pad and pen carefully down beside me.

"The war, you mean?" I asked him.

"No. Not the war. I don't mind the god-damn war. When do you think it's going to stop? The rain?"

It was coming down steadily on the roof of the bunker, like marbles on the stretched skin of a timber drum, the first time I had really noticed it in more than a week. The storm season had been with us for over a month. I had learned to blot it out of my consciousness. The Green Beret, apparently, had not.

"It really worries you, then?"

He twitched. "I don't know. It's enemy rain, I think. It's gook rain. It's against us. All that you can see and all that you can hear and all that you can *feel* is that rain. It gets in everywhere, it's"—he wrapped his arms around himself and shivered—"drowning us.

When do you think it's going to stop? The rain?"

I looked at him for a long time. Then I shook my head. "I don't know," I said quietly. And I picked up my pen and pad again . . .

Now it was hammering down on the roof of the car as I drove toward the garage in Victoria. A few cars flashed past going the other way, their headlights blazing. At the garage, I drove into the repair bay to get the rear end and the taillights fixed, left the keys with them, and took another model out of their hire fleet. A gray Ford sedan. It felt big and unwieldy, but the people from Sam Loong would not be looking for a gray Ford sedan. I drove to Soho.

The red transit van was standing quite abandoned-looking on the cobblestones when I arrived. I parked across the street from the mouth of the alley, switched off the engine and lights, and waited. I knew Grey—he would let them go, but not immediately. I settled back in my seat, lighted a cigarette and watched the smoke curl.

Soho was practically dead around me. The few people who hurried by were swathed in black overcoats, hunchbacked beneath black umbrellas, no more substantial in their presence here than passing ghosts. And the neon signs kept flashing on, red and orange and yellow, advertising their bounty of flesh and sex and danger . . . to whom? Only the rain. Only the clouds. I wondered whether the clouds knew about sex, whether they felt a special thrill when they merged against each other, and perhaps the rain and the lightning were the products of all that. And if they knew about that merging, perhaps they knew about loneliness too, and all the strange, mesmeric fashions it could take. I hoped not. I hoped to God not. For their sake.

God, what's taking them so long?

What's taking them? Ashtray full now. Strange, because it was empty when I started. Cigarette down-dangling between my fingers, singeing the carpet on the gearstick plinth, barely noticed now, sick of the taste of smoke, just lighting them and letting them burn. Expensive habit. Life is an expensive habit. What's taking them so long?

Halfway into my doze, I had a semi-waking dream that a great dark creature was coming toward the car, moving on a jumble of short legs. It wasn't a dream. I jerked upright in my seat, switched the wipers on, and as they sluiced through the water running down the windshield I could see the company of the Sam Loong Puppet Theatre halfway down the road, huddled together as they marched in my direction. They were out of their traditional costumes now, wearing jeans and fleece coats and anoraks, and their black hair was plastered down against their

scalps by the rain, their yellow faces down-
turned. They did not even notice me. About
twenty yards from my car, they hurried
across the road and into the alleyway, up the
wooden stairs which led to their hideaway. I
glanced at my watch. It was one o'clock.

My heart was thumping; one of my hands
went out to the wheel and gripped it tight.

The wind had changed direction. The rain
was striking slantwise all along the road and
spattering, bouncing off the asphalt in a
silver swarm of tiny, broken drops. It took
five minutes for the puppet people to reap-
pear. They were lugging huge packing baskets, just as Charlie had described, just as I
had seen them do in Covent Garden; they
manhandled them down the stairs and loaded
them into the back of the van. The motor
started.

I was just about to reach for my own
ignition key when I noticed something I had
not seen before. I should have guessed, of
course. Grey was a corrupt bastard, but he
was not an idiot. A navy blue Rover had
pulled into the empty space across from me,
just to the side of the alleyway. There were
two short-haired, hard-looking young men
inside. I leaned back into my seat and waited.

The transit van slid out of the alley and
turned left, heading for Oxford Street. Like a
dark blue lizard, the Rover shifted in behind
it. I waited until they were a way down the

street, and then I brought my own car into life and slithered it away from the curb and followed them. The first set of lights almost caught me. I went across on the red, ignoring them.

The closer we got to Oxford Street, the more crowded the roads became. A woman out Saturday shopping in a yellow coat and yellow sou'wester stepped into my lane without looking and, swerving to avoid her, I practically went against the paintwork of the car on my outside. A messenger bike hummed by like a too-large insect. There were horns blaring somewhere far ahead. The red van and the dark blue car wove through the traffic ahead of me like paired dancers. The Rover had been forced too close. I hung to the inside lane, watching.

There was no need for the van to have stopped at the next set of lights. They were only just turning to amber, but the driver slammed on his brakes and Grey's men practically crashed into his back. The two machines hung suspended there like racers at a starting line while the crosstown traffic roared past. I frowned speculatively and idled to a halt ten yards behind them.

My wipers went *tuk tuk tuk* across the windshield. The rain had gone out of my consciousness now, just like in that bunker. All the old tricks coming back now. All the old tricks.

Now the lights were going to amber again
and the transit van was lurching forward,
throwing up spray. It made as if to bypass
Centre Point, continue north—then, without
warning, it made a left into a one-way street
just wide enough to allow it through.

The Rover slowed a moment; I could see
the two men inside consulting frantically,
split-second decision. Follow the van down
there, and the Chams would know they were
being shadowed. The driver put his foot
down. The Rover sped past the turning, up
to the junction at New Oxford Street, took a
left so sharply it slammed across the curb,
and disappeared from sight, hurrying to pick
the transit up again at the far end of the
one-way street.

Me, I stayed behind. I braked sharply—a
taxicab blared at me from the rear—and
pulled up onto the pavement. Sure enough,
half a minute later, the transit van backed
out of the siding into the main road again.

*Nice.* I lighted another cigarette. *Very nice.*

It continued its journey north. I dropped in
three cars behind it, and followed.

*Tuk tuk tuk.*

The West End was left behind. We moved
toward the suburbs. The traffic flowed in a
steady, spray-enveloped river through the
rain. All around us the bright primary colors
of storefront windows and the people walking
by them bled to dusty reds and reddish-

browns and the colors of perpetual autumn.
Then we were farther away from the city
center, and there were neat, tree-lined av-
enues giving way on either side of the main
street, with fences painted green or white
and evenly trimmed hedges and houses with
their fronts pebble-dashed or covered with
rectangular gray-white slabs of artificial stone,
and there were cars parked in the graveled
driveways. The transit van slipped into the
outside lane and took a right, and then we
were climbing. I took a last drag at the
cigarette, tasted the filter burning and
stubbed it out. We were going toward
Hampstead.

High over London it sits, part of the city
and yet separate from it, like a Victorian
monarch on its throne; and if you look at it
from a distance what you can see is the great
sprawl of trees that make up the Heath, and
around and in between that sprawl are tall,
fantastically roofed houses, rows of them,
grand and aloof as chess pieces immobile on
some stone-and-tarmac board. We went
through a street the French had once occupied and left resembling a discreet, overgrown boulevard. We passed a modern
alleyway which looked like a little Italy, and
another one which had remained unchanged
since Shaw's and Dickens's and William
Wilkie Collins's days. The van, ahead of my
scything wipers, began to clamber up through

the narrow side streets, past olde worlde pubs
and trees so old and so massive some of
them blotted out the sky, the light coming
through in flips and starts. I kept my distance, trying to blend into the background
and the pouring rain.

I was already looking, in the highest windows of one of those houses, for drawn
curtains with an Oriental foliage design.
*Find me, Mr. Auden. Find me.*

Getting close. I could feel it.

And then a green and black lorry began
backing out of a side street.

The driver of the van saw it, and the van
accelerated sharply and got around. I put my
foot down on the gas, trying to follow. Too
late. The motor truck had blocked the entire
width of the road. I slammed the brake
down, skidded, practically hitting it, then
jammed my hand down on the horn.

Come on! For God's sake! I kept on hooting.
The lorry stood there, without moving. In his
cab, the driver sat rigid. It was as though he
was in a trance. I steered the car onto the
sidewalk, broke all records getting to the
junction at the top of the street.

The lorry was moving off by now.

The junction was empty. I looked both
ways, straining my eyes against the downpour, trying to pick out some sign, something, anything. Nil, not a trace. Gone. *Damn!*

I slammed my fist against the steering wheel. Outside the car, the wind began to moan like a hunting animal, just as it had done in the temple by the riverside.

# CHAPTER 22

I stopped at a bar in Camden Town on the way back. It didn't have a name anymore, that bar; someone had taken the sign down. The windows were boarded up. But all things considered, the owners had got off lightly. Just across from the narrow car park, where the parade of local shops started, the nearest two small stores had gone to charred rubble, still hot at their centers, sending up trailers of steam against the falling rain. I looked away, bought a paper from the vendor standing in the shelter of the lounge door, went inside. The bar was dimly lit, and it smelled of last night's smoke.

"A Black and White, please. Soda."

I sat in a corner with the newspaper across my knees, flipped past the first six pages on

the riots to the cartoons, took a few goes at
the crossword. Around me, glasses clinked,
and the few other customers talked in whis-
pers. There was a portable television switched
on over the bar. Some news came on. Mobs
clashed with police. The publican walked
over and switched the picture to a gardening
program on Channel 4.

"Witchcraft . . ."

"Sorry?" I said, turning, my mind still half
on the crossword.

The woman sitting with two young men at
the next table, all of them wearing jeans and
anoraks, looked at me and then smiled. "We
were discussing the riots, the return to the
Dark Ages. Perhaps even the resurgence of
witchcraft. It's in your paper."

"Where?"

She took it from me, turned to page eight.
There, in the lower left-hand corner, was a
small eight-line bulletin. Two graves had
been disturbed in a west London cemetery
early last night.

"Oh, Jesus."

"Pardon?" the woman asked.

I took the paper with me across to the bar,
got the publican's attention and pointed to
the television set.

"Could you turn that back to the news?" I
asked.

He scowled at me, finally reached up and
flicked a switch.

Golf results. Jesus!

I waited to see if there was going to be any local, Thames area, news.

It came on and there were more mobs, and then a widow had been stabbed to death in Croydon, and someone had broken the high-dive somersault record, and then—

The graveyard in Shepherd's Bush appeared on the screen. Police stood around the overturned tombstones of Cha Than Ton and Cha Huen Lin. There were two sets of tire tracks nearby. One of them had to be the limousine's. The other?

"Thanks," I told the publican.

I ran through the rain toward my car, holding the newspaper over my head.

The desk sergeant at the Shepherd's Bush station was less than impressed with my press card. No, the detective in charge of the case was not available. Why hadn't I come earlier, with the other reporters? Yes, the bodies had been exhumed for re-examination. Why? They weren't prepared to say yet. No, I could *not* speak to the pathologist. No, I could *not* see whatever they'd uncovered. Two black and two white kids were being herded down toward the cells. The place had no smells, no bright colors, nothing but the echo of long corridors and the subliminal buzzing of the overhead fluorescent lights. I went across the road to a telephone box and began putting in calls to anyone with political muscle I knew, promising favors, calling in old debts, digging deep into the mire of friends of friends of the Chief Commissioner.

Half an hour later, I was sitting in a dry white corridor outside a double swing-door marked PATHOLOGY. A youngish man, in his early thirties perhaps, with shoulder-length blond hair, came through and stopped and looked at me, surprised. My coat was soaked through and my hair was plastered down across my forehead. I brushed it to the side, trying to look like somebody more important. The pathologist smiled.

"Mr. Auden?" He shook my hand, then held out a white surgical mask. "You might need this. Would you like to come inside?"

There were no shadows anywhere in the room. Bright blazing white and the smell of formaldehyde. And this is where it all ends, I thought. In a city of light and darkness and flashing neon and dull orange streetlamps and scuttling people and hurrying cars and rain and smoke and cold, this is where it all ends, in a blinding white windowless cube of a room wherein a man deals with the mechanics of death. I felt as though I were floating, in there. I wished I'd brought a drink with me. I wished I'd brought some mud in on my shoes. The tiles rang beneath my footsteps. In the direct center of the floor there was a trolley.

Lying on the trolley, covered to its waist by a white sheet, was the corpse of a boy in his mid-teens, the face turned slightly toward me. Both feet were protruding from under the sheet and there was a plastic tag around the big toe.

"Him?" I asked the pathologist.

"Glue." He walked over and took hold of the sheet. "Yessiree. Sniffin' glue is the thing ta do. Fifteen years old." He sighed, flipped the sheet over the boy's face and walked back to me.

I could not look away from the trolley. The sheet settled in puffs and flutters until it had molded itself around the contours of the boy's face.

The pathologist took me gently by the sleeve.

"You've got a lot of important friends, I gather," he said, leading me toward what looked like a set of oversized filing cabinets at the far end of the room.

"I wouldn't exactly call them friends. But you were a hard man to get close to half an hour ago. Why are the boys in blue being so uptight?"

"Illegal immigrants? From that part of the world? What do you think?"

"Drugs?"

"Right."

"Did you find any drugs?"

"No." He took hold of the handles of two

adjacent cabinets. "Other things. No trace of drugs. Deep breath, now."

He yanked the cabinets open. They came forward on their rollers with an abrupt rasping sound. Then silence.

"Cha Than Ton and Cha Huen Lin," the pathologist said. "Mortal remains of." My eyes were watering.

I tried to laugh, plucked at the mask I was wearing. "Perhaps I should have worn this over my eyes."

"Not very pretty, but that's what we all look like underneath our peachy complexions and our big blue eyes. The epidermis," he intoned, "is the ultimate cosmetic." He shoved the cabinets closed.

I was still gulping for air a little. "Were those . . . those little scraps of yellow . . . ?"

"The parchmenty-looking things? Flesh, yes. A few traces of scalp, some with tufts of hair attached." He began moving me away toward some other, smaller, cabinets.

"I don't know," I said. "I was expecting bare bones, funhouse skeletons."

He nodded. "It depends on a lot of factors. The toughness of the casket, for one. And then, of course, there's the drainage. If the corpse is buried over clay, it will have rotted totally in the space of two years. Over gravel, however, the ground is never wet for long, and some of the flesh will simply petrify."

"It certainly petrified me."

"Yes. I'm sorry."

"How much were the caskets disturbed?"

"Very heavily. Whoever disturbed them was really extremely determined."

"Witchcraft? Like the papers have been saying?"

"That's the line the police have been feeding them. Myself, I wouldn't even like to hazard a guess."

He slid open one of the filing drawers and took out a plastic bag, emptied the contents into his palm.

"They were each wearing one of these," he said.

Two golden rings. Each engraved with a continuous line of tiny skulls.

"And these"—he pulled out another bag—"around their necks."

He dangled them in front of me.

On tangled chains, two golden pendants, each with a purple gem set in it, turning, flashing, cats' eyes in the dark, turning, turning . . .

*The room went away from me with a sickening diagonal jolt. I could feel my legs giving way. I was back in the dream again, back in the holy shrine, the* dinh. *And there was the idol. And there was the slab. The body was lying on it, a woman's emaciated body, trying to get words up like bubbles through the lava of her pain. And there were the other people, crowded around her, and two of them, a man and a woman, were holding something between them. My eyes fastened on their necks. They were wearing those same two pendants.*

*Then I was in the telephone booth, and the voice was coming at me.*

"Mr. Auden?"

"Mr. Thomas Auden?"

I tried to kick and fight away from it. Swim, laddie, swim for the blinding white light. Swim for the little white room which stands like a vortex in the whirlpool of our dreams. White light. No shadows. White light.

I came back.

"Mr. Auden?"

The pathologist had grabbed hold of my coat and stopped me falling. He was struggling to get me onto a stool. I found the strength somewhere to help him.

"That better?"

"Thank you. Christ!" I put my face in my hands, then ripped the mask away, gasping.

The pathologist was trying to take my pulse, but he was shaking too much. The expression on his face was one of white sick terror. "It's my fault," he blurted. "I'm sorry. I'm really sorry. The corpses. I forget that people don't react—"

I brushed him aside. I was all cold sweat and trembling. "No," I said. "No, it wasn't the corpses. God knows, I've seen enough of those things."

It took a while to reassure him. He went and fetched me a glass of water, and when I sipped it, it tasted of formaldehyde.

"Are you okay now?"

"Yeah. I think so." I put my finger and thumb at the corners of my eyes and took a few more deep breaths. The pendants had been returned to their bag and shut away. "Did you find anything else?"

"In the coffins?"

"Uh-huh."

"A few shreds of clothing. Something interesting there," the pathologist said.

"How interesting?"

"Sent them down to forensics. Are you sure you're okay?"

"Positive. Go on."

"Nothing of value on the man's clothing, but on the woman's ... the original fabric was brushed denim. The boys in the lab, however, found microscopic traces of linen, cotton, various synthetic fabrics."

"After this long?"

"Modern technology."

"Well," I said, carefully standing up, "hooray for modern technology. Is that it?"

"No. I found traces of the same fibers in the woman's nasal cavities and among the remains of her scalp."

"Is it significant?"

"That kind of concentration, just before she died? I'd say a working environment."

I looked at him, squinting.

"An illegal immigrant?" he said. "In a workplace full of airborne specks of fiber?" He smiled. "You're a journalist, Mr. Auden. You can work it out for yourself."

# CHAPTER 23

And the rain came down.

I drove through it, through the night that was closing down over London like the lid of a gray glass tomb, until I reached the maze of alleys I was looking for; then I drove through them, the tires kangarooing on the cobblestones, my headlights picking out the walls of old pre-war factories, like docked rotting ships in the gathering darkness, gone to dandelions and moss. They were all quiet except one. I parked across from it. It was a single-story building with gaping cracks in the brickwork and an asbestos roof patched with tarpaper. A single chimney protruded. The high, square, barred frost-glass windows glowed with electric light. I sat where I was a moment, lighted a fresh cigarette, half-glad

that somebody else was still working on a
Saturday evening. Then I got out of the car
and hurried through the rubbish on the wet,
loose stones.

The incredible noise hit me as I opened the
door and stepped inside. Sewing machines,
about three dozen of them, set in ranks
across the shop floor—they were hammering
so loudly even the rain on the roof could not
be heard and each of them but one abandoned one was being operated by an Asian girl
from mid-teens into early thirties. I picked
out an Oriental face bent over an old black
Singer and pondered a moment.

Then one of the women noticed me, then
two, then three. Faces gone pallid and etched
with sootlike shadows stared up at me. Brown
eyes lost their glaze and became alarmed.
Then everyone remembered themselves and
looked away. I walked across the bare boards
to the door at the far end. The tempo of the
sewing machines had not subsided once.

Her name was Mrs. Harris; it said so on
the plate at the front of her neat desk in the
tiny outer office, where the green carpet
began. She was in her middle fifties with
red-dyed hair pulled back from her face with
an elastic band. Her head was turned away
from me. She was quite motionless, so engrossed in what she was watching that she
did not even notice the machine noise wash
over her when I stepped in through the door.

The partitions to the inner office were plyboard to waist-height, then frosted glass the rest of the way. And on the frosted glass a shadow show was taking place, two human figures, one tiny and female, the other large, pressed behind her. I could see Mrs. Harris's reflection in the glass. Mrs. Harris was smiling like a benign *duenna*.

Her eyes moved. She saw my reflection in the glass, whirled around, face already turned to stone, palm moving for the buzzer at the corner of her desk. The lights in Scully's office clicked off.

"Too late," I told her.

"For *what*? Who are you?"

"Not the police."

"The pop group or the Metropolitan? You just barged in here."

"I didn't barge. I walked. My name's Tom Auden. Mr. Scully knows me."

"*Barged* in," she said.

She studied me carefully, looking me up and down. She flicked a switch on the desk intercom and said efficiently, "Mr. Scully? There's a Mr. Auden here to see you." A few seconds later, the lights behind the frost-glass came back on. The large shadow was seated behind its desk. The tiny one was standing near the door, head bowed.

"If you'll just take a seat," said Mrs. Harris, indicating the farthest one away from her.

As soon as I had settled down, the tiny shadow began moving in a long continuous scurry which took her through the outer office, revealing her as a thin pretty Asian girl of about eighteen, leaving both doors slammed behind her as she disappeared into the workshop. She was wearing a blue nylon smock like all the other women, but it was open at the front, and the middle two buttons of her blouse had been done up wrongly.

She was trying not to cry.

I felt my gorge rise.

I looked at Mrs. Harris. She was intently scribbling something on her blotter, but smiling.

"You just watch?" I asked her.

The smile grew wider.

"Does he know you watch?"

Her face pursed into a blank, concentrated frown. "Mr. Scully will see you now," she said, not looking up.

I went into his office. It stank of his sweat and I tried not to look at him at first. Two years ago, when the drink still got me really blurry, I had fallen in for a short time with some crowd at an after-hours drinking club in Soho. Maxwell Scully had been one of them.

The office was well soundproofed. It had sepia walls and a thick Wilton carpet. A badly-forged Constable, two photographs of yachts, some kind of certificate and a girlie calendar hung on the walls. The blinds were drawn. There was a drinks cabinet at the far side of the room. The light bulb in the center of the ceiling had an art deco shade around it, completely out of place.

Huge and bearded and going bald, Maxwell Scully shifted impatiently in his leather seat. He had the flushed, sweaty look of an overweight man who tried to take too much exercise. He would probably die of a heart attack in the squash court of some unfussy country club, and it was far too good a way for him to die.

He gave me a massive, warmthless smile.

"Hello, Thomas!"

"How's the wife, Scully?"

"Oh, shut up, Thomas."

"How're the children?"

"I bought my wife a brand-new BMW last week."

"I'll bet she was thrilled."

"Of course she was. You're a bore, Thomas."

"Perhaps an anonymous phone call . . ."

"Get *lost*!"

"No."

I went across to the drinks cabinet and snatched out a glass, then the bottle of scotch.

"Put that bloody down! You've got no manners!"

I continued to pour. Scully leaned back in

his seat and chewed his thumbnail, eyeing
me with a bored kind of anger.

"Help yourself to a drink, Thomas," he
said. *"Oh, thank you very much, Maxwell. I
think I'll have a scotch*. Go right ahead,
Thomas. Be my guest. Fine, spill some on the
carpet! I'll buy a new one." His grin returned. "I will, you know. *You* couldn't do
that."

"Wonderful. Did you get inside her?"

"Shut up, Thomas."

"What do you think of her as? A she or an
it?"

"Hearts and bloody flowers, Thomas! It's
one of the perks of management. What do
you think it matters to her, either way?"

"Makes you feel good when she goes all
rigid, right?"

Bolt upright in his chair now. "I'm going
to throw you bloody out!"

"Better still," I said, "call the police."

His color phased toward purple for an
instant. Then he relaxed, leaned back in his
chair, and gradually began to chuckle until
finally it was coming from deep in his chest,
his eyes were running. He waggled a finger
at me with an odd-looking ring on it.

"Know what this is? Freemasons. Last
year. I'm going up in the world, Thomas
Auden. Some day, far too high for stupid
pricks like you to touch me." He fished a
handkerchief out of his pocket and dabbed

at his cheeks. "In the meantime," he said and smiled, "what can I do to help the little people?"

Do you know, I thought, how degrading it is having to deal with people like you? I topped up the glass.

"Well?" he asked.

There was an insect trapped in the art deco lampshade, tapping feebly, trying to get out.

"Well?" Scully asked.

"I'm looking for a link with the past. A bridge, if you like. I'm looking for someone who remembers a woman, might have worked in one of the shops around here."

"Illegal, this woman?"

I nodded. "Name of Cha Huen Lin. Vietnamese."

"They're not illegal, clod. They're refugees."

"Not this one."

"No?"

"1971."

"Are you out of your—"

"I want you to talk to your own staff," I broke in. "I want you to phone every shop owner in the district, get them to do the same. There's got to be one person who remembers her."

"Fourteen years, Thomas."

"I can count."

"Do you know what kind of a turnover there is in fourteen years?"

"Try," I said.

He began to chuckle again, quietly now. "You know what you sound like to me? You sound like a man who's drowning."

I looked at the insect in the lampshade. "Perhaps."

"Then fuck you, Thomas. Drown."

That struck him as very hilarious, the way it would strike a twelve-year-old schoolboy. The laughter took hold of him and he bent slightly forward in his chair, one hand against the desk, cheeks going red. A few strands of hair flapped across his bald patch. I sighed, sipped from my glass, looked away. Gazed around that boring little office, which echoed and rebounded Scully's braying noises. Such a small man. For someone so physically large, so ursine, such a tiny man.

A straight-backed chair stood in front of his desk. I put down my glass, walked to it, and leaned on it. And began talking, very softly.

"Scully, you'd better sober up your attitude. You'd better stop laughing at me. Because, listen, you may think I'm just a burned-out old has-been, but I was up for the Pulitzer once. Did you know that? I scooped the Los Angeles awards two years running, in my time. I was a great journalist once. And there may not be much of that left, but somewhere deep inside me there's a little quiet reserve, still there, and all it needs to tap it is for you to throw me out of here. I swear it, Scully. You'll never reach that peak you're climbing for. You'll never reach that safe place. If I need to, I'll spend the final years of my life exposing you and every other scum who lives off people's fear and their sweat. But especially you. Start believing it, Scully—I'll do it.''

He was still grinning hugely, damp-faced, but now he was looking straight at me, eyes filled with intrigued surprise.

"I'll have you killed first," he said.

"You wouldn't be that stupid."

"You're bluffing."

"Like to take that risk?"

I went away and picked up my glass.

"Look," Scully said from behind me.

It was a nice glass. I tipped it so that it caught the light.

"Okay," Scully said, "I'll do it, but on this condition. When you've got what you want, you walk out of this office and I never see you or hear of you again. You see me walking down the street, you cross to the other side. You walk into a bar and I'm there, you step back out and don't return. I'm doing it this way because it's easier, Auden. You go back on me, and I will kill you."

I finished off the drink, dropped the empty glass on the carpet, and went back into the outer office, taking all the stink of that man with me.

Mrs. Harris was still scribbling.

I made myself comfortable. The newspaper was still in my raincoat pocket, damp and crumpled, spongy-feeling; I laid it carefully across my lap and opened it to the crossword.

"Do you have a pen?" I asked Mrs. Harris.

"No."

There were seven pens beside her on the desk.

I looked at my watch. When I looked at it again, only nine minutes had passed, and only six minutes the next time after that. The noise of the sewing machines came like a muted heartbeat through the outer door.

Mrs. Harris began typing, slamming on the keys.

I scratched behind my ear and stared at her until she decided to do something quieter.

The telephone rang and she answered it, jotted something down.

When it rang again, the time was six-thirty. She made some more jottings, then replaced the receiver and went to get her coat. She walked out without even a backward glance.

Two minutes after she had gone, the light on the intercom blinked on. I walked across and flicked a switch. "The watchbird's gone, Scully. How are you doing with Cha Huen Lin?"

He switched off without replying.

Only three of his staff passed through the

doors and were questioned in all that time. One of them was the Oriental girl. The other two were older Asian women, gaunt with fatigue, who had probably been living in this country fifteen years or more. They disappeared into the office, one by one, and I could see their shadows bobbing and shaking their heads. None of the interviews lasted longer than a minute.

I was hungry now. I went to Mrs. Harris's desk, rummaged through the drawers, found an apple and a half-filled packet of digestive biscuits. The core went quickly in the waste bin. I only managed two of the biscuits, though. My stomach was jumping.

The phone went off like a volcano in Scully's office. I heard him snatch it up; his voice filtered indistinctly through the partition.

*Got it!*

My stomach flipped again. I tasted apple in my mouth.

Scully put the phone down.

His shadow moved toward the door and opened it, and he was standing there, rings under his eyes now, staring at me balefully.

"Well?" I asked.

"Her name is Isela Shapoor, a supervisor at McKean's shop. She's waiting for you now outside Goldhawk Road station. Good-bye, Thomas Auden," he said.

I went directly past the thin pretty Asian girl on the way out. She was in between two homelier women, and neither of them were looking at her, their shoulders angled slightly away; she was trapped on the desert island of her loneliness. There were only dark smudges under her eyes to remind you of her tears. The workshop lights reflected dully off her skin, and already her prettiness was transforming, becoming something false and lusterless and puttylike until, given time, it would come to resemble Mrs. Harris's face.

*No deals*.

I went out into the biting cold and the rain.

*No deals with bastards like Scully*. But, of course, the girl was illegal. If I exposed the sweat shop, who would suffer most? Scully, with his money and his Freemasonry and his brand-new BMW? Or her? The rise and rise of Maxwell Scully. He would be rubbing shoulders with titled heads and captains of industry one day, and there was not a damned thing I could do to stop it.

I took a last glance back at the building with its glowing windows, standing like a fortress among ramparts and battlements and barricades of age-old shadows. Then I went to find Isela Shapoor. It was seven twenty-five.

I never managed to keep that appointment. A hundred yards from the station, my gray

Ford sedan turned into the jeep, and as the impact took it, it was flying, rolling over, over, and I was spinning once again into a darkness deeper than the night.

# CHAPTER 24

It had no lights, the truck that hit me. It came out of the side street like something heavy falling, ramming my car broadside with direct precision. *Deliberate* precision. It had been no accident. I could remember it, weeks later, as though the whole event were a meticulously choreographed dance move, performed and reperformed and repeated in fluid slow motion.

And somehow, I did not die.

God, how I wanted to die.

The rain was splashing on my face when I came to. It was getting in slantwise past the few remaining edges of the windshield, and my head was angled back and to the side as though to receive it, Holy water, washing my sins away. It was bringing me back to consciousness; and it was sluicing the blood from my face.

I started, blindly, raising one hand to my eyes—then I heard the motor purring, close beside me, and froze. I could hear the exhaust puttering and the rapid *tick-tick-tick* of the timing, and the throbbing of some large, powerful engine as it idled no more than a couple of yards from my face. My neck was burning with pain by now, as was the side of my left leg. I dared not move them. I opened my eyes just a crack, keeping otherwise perfectly still.

The van was there.

The bright red transit van of the Sam Loong Puppet Theatre, a yellow face peering at me out of the side window, almost close enough to touch. How long had they been there? I wish I knew. The van hung there a moment longer, like a bright red bird inspecting something it had thought was food, then sped away into the darkness.

*Go*, I thought, *tell her the news. Tell her your last lead is gone. Tom Auden is dead*. My leg hurt awfully where it had slammed against the gearstick. I shifted it, tried to sit up straight.

The car was leaning on its side. Only the seat belt was holding me in place. There was a half-burned cigarette glowing down on the passenger side, out of reach—and the smell of gasoline was strong.

Still watching that tiny spot of glowing orange, I reached for the door. It was stuck. I unbuckled myself very carefully, clinging with my free arm to the seat. I tried to clamber across the dashboard and out through the shattered windshield. My left leg was like a block of iron. My foot slipped, wedged itself somewhere beneath the steering column. The fear inside me reared itself up like a great black stallion, ready to batter at me with its hooves. Panic and you'll die, laddie. Don't let it happen. I reached for the windshield and took firm hold of its rubber lip. I tried to ease myself out of the car. My leg was still trapped. I got my right foot down next to it, hoping I could lever myself free. Nothing happened. I closed my eyes, kept on tugging.

Something in my knee popped a little. I stopped pulling before I really seriously injured myself, but there were tears starting up in my eyes now, there was sweat breaking out all over my face, chilling as it touched the air, mingling with the rain. And there was salt in my eyes, and salt corroding my lips, and above all that the smell of gasoline. I raised my right foot and kicked at the steering column. Twice, three times, four. Then five. Then six.

My left leg came free.

When the car took fire, it was quietly but solidly, all at once, like all the nozzles of a gas stove bursting into blue, then yellow flame. I was on the opposite pavement by then, sitting there rubbing my leg.

The entire street was washed with moving, flowing light. The rain caught and reflected it, as though it were raining fire. Where it hit the burning car, columns of steam began to rise.

So there I was in a telephone booth at the corner of two streets again. No ring of skulls engraved into the glass this time. No insane voices coming at me out of the receiver. The car was still shallowly burning back along the road. It had taken me the best part of three minutes to limp this far. I leaned against the glass, with the rain pouring in small floods down the outside, and gasped for breath, and thought, and thought.

How long had they been following me? To Spellbrook? To the house the Chas had lived in? *All the time?* It should have been impossible in that damned bright red van of theirs but—*she's a mistress of disguise*, Ginny Hawkins had said. I had been dumped in front of those two gravestones in Shepherd's Bush, and come the next morning the graves had been disturbed. I had lain there half dead in the road, and they had been there, watching me. Just perhaps some of those puppeteers, those servants of the madwoman, were up to a little conjuring, an imitation of mythical powers. It made me remember something

from far back in my past. There was a game
I used to play, as a little boy. . . .

I picked up the receiver and began to dial.

In the game, in the bright middle of winter
when the snow lay like an unruffled white
sea to the horizon every morning when I
woke, I would pretend I was a treasure
hunter following a trail. Usually it was my
father's, the deep, regular imprints of his
boots leading in a straight line from our gate
toward the town. They were like the echoes
of his presence. And I, my heart pounding,
would race along behind them, knowing today was the day I would find the treasure.
But as I drew closer to the center of the
town, another line of footprints would inter-
sect my father's, then another. Until, by the
time I reached the square, all that remained
was an anthill maze of prints against the
white. . . .

The phone at the other end began to ring.

Someone picked it up and said hello, but I
could barely hear him against the row of
background voices and jukebox music, the
clatter of pool balls, the electronic whining
of a games machine. I asked if Johnny Michaels was there and, yes, he did still inhabit
that particular club every Saturday night.
Who wanted him?

"A friend," I said.

"What kind of friend?"

"The kind who saved his hide once. A writer. He'll remember."

I waited, listening to the static on the line and the babble at the other end. A few people were singing, out of tune but with bags of heart. The club was miles away in the East End of London, but listening, I could smell the panatella smoke, feel the press of bodies, taste the beer and whiskey in my empty mouth. I shivered, in my phone box, tried to peer out through the flooded panes. The pain spread up from my neck, and my head began to pound.

Johnny Michaels came abruptly onto the line.

"Mr. Auden?"

I smiled at the sound of his Cockney voice. "It's me, Johnny."

"This is—how did you know I'd be here?"

"Not that difficult a guess."

He laughed. "I suppose not. Anyway, it's good to hear from you. How are you?"

"Less than good."

"Really?"

"Really," I said.

He must have noticed something in the tone of my voice, because he became puzzled and serious after that, the ebullience suddenly gone. A woman came close to the receiver—pretty drunk, telling a joke—and he shushed her and moved her away. He waited there, listening.

"You remember," I asked him, "last time we met, after you were released, you said if I ever—"

"Needed a favor? Yes, Mr. Auden. Sure. Anything."

"A couple of favors, in fact."

"Anything, like I said. I owe you."

"I don't suppose you'd be involved in what might be called criminal activities anymore."

"Not me."

"But I'll bet you know some people who are."

I could practically hear the smile crack across his face. "Ye-es . . ."

"Two favors, then. I need—" I stopped, thought. Something stirred in the back of my mind. The dream. The dying woman. The Vietnamese crowded around her, the Chas with their pendants. Holding a bundle between them. The blanket slipped slightly away and—

No. No good. It began to fade.

But that was not the whole of it. *Following me. Following.* I was their last lead over a trail fifteen years cold. They had tried Sandy and Stuart and Peter, and none of them had helped, and so they had discarded those three men and come, finally, to me. What was I supposed to remember? What was I supposed to have seen? I didn't know. That was the biggest joke of all. The jeep, the land mine, the six hours of amnesia. I simply didn't know.

"I need a car, Johnny. An automatic. One of my legs is hurt. And . . ."

I faltered there. Two years as a journalist in Vietnam, ten times that many as a trained reporter, and I had always remained simply that, a reporter. Never once, ever, stepped over the line. Not even on that morning in Plieku when the Vietcong were within inches of overrunning the position I was based at. Not even during the last days of the siege at Khe Sanh.

It was time now to cross that line.

"A gun, Johnny," I said. "I need a gun."

# CHAPTER 25

Isela Shapoor was listed in the telephone directory, and easy enough to find. She lived alone in one of those tiny two-up, two-down houses the councils had thrown up in the sixties, and she was so confident that, when she answered the door, she did not even bother to fix the safety chain. She stumbled back into the hallway when she saw the gun, and I followed her in, keeping the revolver trained squarely on her face.

"Get your coat," I told her.

"Who *are* you?"

"A dead man. A hit-and-run truck victim. Get your coat."

And she was nothing. Just a tired, middle-aged Asian spinster, streaks of gray in her black bun of hair, lines in her face so deep they might have been chiseled there. Just a small, weak link in someone else's chain. I remembered the sight of that truck coming at me, and couldn't find it in myself to feel sorry for her.

There was a small statuette of the Buddha in her hallway.

I asked her if she drove, and, yes, she did. We were going to see the man she had told of my destination, the man who had ordered my death.

London is like a brick wall with damp rot on the far side, where the rot keeps coming through and being patched up, and then appearing somewhere else. You walk down a beautiful, immaculate Georgian street, turn a bend, and on the same street find yourself entering a slum. You wander past dozen upon dozen of condemned Victorian hovels and suddenly find, at the center of them, a row of rebuilt dream homes with expensive cars parked tidily outside. Good areas and bad areas lean against each other like pencils crammed into a jar, there are no strict dividing lines. And driving through them, you feel that everything is stroboscoped, coming to you in flashes—good, bad, old, new, order and decay, one after the other, flashing.

Isela Shapoor wasn't making a great deal of conversation, so I reached across, keeping the gun on her, and flicked on the radio. The riots were still going on. You could not pinpoint them now; the rain had doused any chance of fire. But they were out there. You could feel them, out there.

The car crawled to a stop outside a massive, ancient house on the borders of Kensington, in one of those gray areas that can't make up their mind whether they are going respectable or squalid. The house had four stories and a basement, and there were several cracked window panes that I could see, and a roof that looked as though a jumbo jet had skimmed it. Faces were engraved into the stonework around the door. Half animal, half human, blind eyes staring at me, mouths wide open over timeless screams. There was an unwalled front garden, all rubble and dandelions now. Isela Shapoor started crossing it rather too quickly, and I pulled back the hammer of the gun.

She stopped at the sound of the click. She had been driving confidently enough, but now her legs were practically giving way.

"Don't play up on me now," I said. I glanced at the house. It was completely dark. "Go on." I motioned with the gun toward the front door.

While she was teetering toward the bell, I flattened myself against the wall, just out of sight.

It took a long time for a light to come on in the hallway. Even then, it was the very dimmest of lights, the merest ocher whisper against the dark. I waited, rain sliding down, dripping off the barrel of my gun. And then the door moved open a crack. And I was there, shoving Isela Shapoor ahead of me, thrusting the gun forward as I went inside. It ended up against the throat of a young Vietnamese man, somewhere about five-foot-seven tall. Not a Cham, an authentic Oriental Vietnamese of the kind I'd seen every day for two years. He had longish hair and a black mustache, a short-sleeved shirt he had not bothered to button up. There was an automatic handgun jammed into the waistband of his trousers. His eyes became huge. I could feel his Adam's apple moving underneath my revolver's barrel.

"That thing. Get rid of it."

He lifted the handgun out with two fingers, very politely, and dropped it, kicking it away into a corner.

Two more young Viet men appeared at the top of the stairs, both of them armed. They froze when they saw me. Had no choice. Shapoor and their friend were walled between us.

I applied a little extra to the pressure on their friend's throat.

Both of their guns came tumbling down the stairway.

"Where is he?" I said.

All of them had turned to stone.

"Your boss? Which room?"

It was an involuntary gesture on Isela Shapoor's part. If she had not been afraid she would never have done it—but for an instant, her eyes left my gun, glanced toward a closed door at the rear of the hallway. The young man in the short-sleeved shirt lashed out and cracked her across the cheek.

The two at the top of the stairs began to move. I tightened my grip on the trigger.

Everyone turned to stone again except Isela Shapoor, who was hugging her mouth trying to stop the bleeding. I turned her and the young man around and propelled them down the hallway.

The house sprawled around us like the long-abandoned shell of some vast, untidy mollusk. Bare boards clattered underneath our feet. There were no shades on the lights, no ornaments or furniture at all. The wallpaper had faded to colorlessness, pattern gone. The paint on the woodwork had mostly flaked away. And a draft, starting somewhere near the top of the house, was being funneled down the stairwell, rattling at the door latches like an intruder testing every lock. I don't know what I had imagined, but it wasn't this.

There was another faint light showing from underneath the rear door. No sound came from inside. I gestured for Shapoor to turn the handle—when she had done it, I shoved the both of them inside, keeping them firmly in front of me. They were my shield.

And I needed it. There were four more young Vietnamese men in there, kneeling, pistols trained.

There was the shallow report of a silencer. A bullet plunged into the wall six inches from my head. I grabbed hold of the young man, pulled him back against me, arm around his throat, gun wedged firmly underneath his jawbone.

There were no more wild shots.

My eyes worked to adjust to the scant light in the room. It was a vast room, empty and drafty as the rest, stretching back to a bay of French windows which opened on to a garden as tangled, in the darkness, as a Jackson Pollock vision of hell. There was something at the back, framed against the windows, where the light from the single bulb practically petered out. A dark, hunched shape. Something sitting in a chair. Someone . . .

Someone sitting in a wheelchair.

I aimed my gun at it. The other four dropped theirs.

The shape in the wheelchair did not move an inch.

"I'm waiting," I said.

I was at the center of a dimly lit tableau. My nerves began to jangle.

"We could be here all night," I said.

"You are," came a voice from the far end of the room, "Mr. Thomas Auden?"

And something curled up inside me at the sound of that voice. The words came irregularly spaced, as though with enormous effort. There was a sandpaper quality to them, dry and flat and painful. I had heard that kind of voice many times, fifteen years ago—it had come from men burned, blasted, hideously wounded, to the point where mouths barely functioned and lungs rasped one against the other and the throat was reduced to no more than a brittle, inflexible tube. Blood coming out with every sentence. Eyes wild with pain. All of a sudden, I did not want to take a closer look at that man in the wheelchair.

"Show me—your left hand," came the voice.

I let go of the young man's throat, held my left hand up toward the light.

"Thank—you. Now, please unbutton your collar."

I worked at the first two buttons.

"Lower—please."

I went halfway down, then yanked aside my coat and shirt, exposing my neck, my chest.

"No medallions," I said. "No rings with skulls engraved around them. You've made a goddamn big mistake, haven't you?"

"Perhaps," said the voice. "That depends—what exactly you are."

\*  \*  \*

I told him the whole story, starting with the *dinh* in Vietnam, going on to Mallory's death, the phone call, the trail which had led me through all the realms of violence and insanity until finally I had found him. He had sent the others out of the room by now, we were alone, he by the French windows, myself still by the door. If he listened without moving, I was sure it was because he could not move. I kept the gun trained on him all the while, just in case. And I tried to make his features out. It was impossible. In the barely present light, he was no more than a murky silhouette.

When I had finished, he paused for a while, then emitted what I suppose, for him, was a sigh. He murmured something to himself in his own language.

"Do you believe in curses, Mr. Auden?"

Yes, I believed in curses.

"Come closer—if you will."

I kept the gun ahead of me and slowly walked across the room.

"Fourteen years ago," he was saying, "in the few short months after the deaths of Mrs. Cha and her husband—my family members were killed in a series of terrible—accidents."

I was closer to him now. His features began to resolve themselves.

"My mother, first," he was saying. "She was—hit by a car and dragged underneath it for practically a quarter of a mile. My eldest brother suffered—a similar fate. My youngest brother happened across some parkland at the same time as an Alsatian. It tore his throat out. And I . . ."

I stopped within six feet of him. I could see him clearly now. Only his voice seemed alive in that whole body. Only his eyes seemed alive in that whole face. The rest of him . . . his hands were no more than claws, ending in black stubs where his fingernails used to be. His face was completely hairless, shriveled to a mass of scar tissue, blotched horribly in places, with a crooked gash that had replaced his mouth, and lashless eyelids so mangled they looked scarcely capable of blinking.

"I," he said, "was in our old house—the night that my father, drunk, out of his mind with grief, fell asleep with his brandy bottle, next to an open fire. I was fifteen at the time."

Something moved inside me, staring at his face. The hideousness of it. The warped, mangled caricature of what had once been human features. *In the dream, inside the dinh . . . We stepped inside the compound. We saw the dying woman on the slab, saw the people gathered around her. The Chas were there, wearing their pendants. They were holding a bundle between them. The bundle moved slightly. The blanket slipped away. Stuart Rawlinson gasped, dropped his camera—*

My focus returned to the man in the wheelchair.

"Are you all right?"

"I think so. Is there another chair around here?"

"Only mine."

I settled down in front of him on my haunches, so that my face was practically level with his and my gun was pointed at his chest. He looked different at that angle, larger. You could almost see the outlines of where, unscathed, he might have grown into a healthy man one year short of thirty; almost trace in the full Oriental features and the cap of straight black hair. Perhaps he was aware of it himself. Perhaps that diagram of what he might have been hung with him like a shadow throughout every waking day—and stalked, fully realized, through his solitary dreams.

There was nothing youthful even about his eyes. Dark brown and bottomless, they seemed as crippled as the rest of him.

My mouth ached with the need for a drink.

"Why do you not," he said, "put the gun down? Do you—honestly think I can harm you?"

I shrugged. "You're my insurance against the boys out there in the hallway. Now, why don't you tell me what happened before the accidents, when you first encountered Mrs. Cha?"

His eyes closed painfully for a moment. He gave another of those rattly sighs.

"It was my father—not myself," he said. "As I pointed out, I was—fifteen at the time. I hung on the periphery of my father's world. And so, I could only at that time make out—*part* of what was going on. The rest I pieced together later, from the testimony of those who survived. I have had—"

"A lot of time to think about it. I know the feeling. Go on."

"My father," he began, "was, back in Vietnam, a great man. Very wealthy and very powerful. But benign. A Buddhist—Mr. Auden. A true believer—of the old school. He was forever—putting his wealth to uses of great philanthropic effect. The number of poor he helped, the orphans he pulled in off the street. The refugees. You would have cried to see it. But long before 1971 he—fell into conflict with an altogether wealthier and— greater man. A corrupt and dangerous official of the Saigon government. We were forced—to flee the country. My family—went to Paris first—but the bureaucrat had contacts there. And so we came to London.

"Even here there—were poor, refugees. My father could not curtail his—old habits. If an immigrant wanted a loan—our house was the place to come. If anyone was having trouble with his landlord, or needed a job, or medicine for his sick child—the same. It is perhaps a measure of the—loyalty and respect he commanded—that the men who tried so zealously to defend me just now, are the sons and nephews of my father's original employees.

"In addition, he was an extremely learned man. When the house went up in flames, fifteen thousand books and scrolls went with it, many of them—ancient and in their original languages. He knew more about our culture, at the moment of his death, more about the roots and history of Eastern religions—than many of those who call themselves 'priests.' Mrs. Cha first came to him in the middle of November—of that year. One month and one year, so it now transpires, after you crossed paths with your land mine.

"She had come about a child. Her and—her husband's child so she claimed, though in the light of later conclusions—my father began to suspect something different. They had just arrived, illegally, from Vietnam. The child was seriously ill and—had been so from birth. Something congenital. I never discovered precisely what. There was no way the Chas could make contact with a doctor through the—conventional channels. So they came to my father instead. He found a doctor for them, went himself to the home where they lived. He came back—badly shaken. The child, so far as I could—make out at that time was—mentally as well as physically ill. Even at that age, I remember it puzzled me why my father—should bother to call at the house instead of simply—leaving it in the hands of the hired physician. It proved soon after that—for the very first time in his life—he had no real interest in the child at all. It was the supposed parents he was interested in. As I said, Mr. Auden, a very—educated, knowledgeable man. He had recognized the pendants and the rings. How much do you know about the Chamic people?"

I explained to him what I had read in the book in Virginia Hawkins's library. His eyelids fluttered down—his version of a nod.

"You know more, then, than ninety-nine percent of Western people. And yes, your assumption that the Chams had their own *thuggee* cult was right. They called themselves—the *kalai*. The children of the goddess Kali. They were, in their heyday, at the right hand of the Chamic warlords. They sat among the kingdom's ministers, held sway in the temples, the armies, even in the courts. And yet, always beneath an impenetrable cloak—of secrecy. You will find no reference to them in Western literature nor—barely any mention of them in the writings of the East. Among all my father's fifteen thousand rare and precious books, I doubt whether there was more—than one mention. That single mention, however, was enough. My father knew of the *kalai*."

"And?"

"And . . . the cult was, *is*, ruled by a priestess, the office being passed in direct line from mother to eldest daughter, majority being reached—at the age of seventeen. There is a ceremony, of course, to initiate the newcomer. It involves the sacrifice of goats, the putting on of special garments—and most important, the gift of a certain rare piece of jewelry. The—badge of office, one might say. My father knew all this. He was an intelligent man. And into his keen—intelligent brain, questions began to come.

"Question: why should two officials of the *kalai* cult leave their country—travel many thousands of miles—simply to seek medical help for one girl child? Answer: the child is the next in line, the 'priestess expectant.'

"Question: if the child is here, and Mrs. Cha is merely an official of the cult, then why is its real mother, the current priestess, not with it? Answer: the mother is dying or already dead. The woman you saw on the slab, Mr. Auden.

"Question: if the child is the only one left in the line of *kalai* priestesses—or else they would not be bothering to save it—where is the ceremonial jewelry? Where is the Necklace? Answer: it is here in England, in the possession of the guardians of the child."

*In the dream—*

"Hold it, backtrack a minute," I said, putting my free hand to my temple.

*In the dream, something glittered around the dying woman's throat. Something very bright.*

"You know nothing of the Necklace?" he asked, faintly surprised.

He could have been there all night, waiting for an answer.

"Little is known—" he said, and he closed his eyes again, the strain of talking so long beginning to wear on him. "Little is known of its history or even its appearance, save that it originally came from India, was fashioned in the Bronze Age, fourteen hundred years before the birth of Christ. In empirical terms, it is no more than an almost worthless bangle, fashioned from bronze and semiprecious stones. But to the priestess of the *kalai*—it is a vital part of her magic, she cannot be fully ordained without it. And to a collector, a museum—absolutely priceless. My father—so holy until then—fell into the *samyojana*, the fetter, of worldly greed. Perhaps the close presence of that evil Necklace warped his mind. He decided to extort it from the Chas."

"He threatened to turn them over to the police?"

"Exactly. He gave them three days in which to comply. At the end of that time, no answer forthcoming, he went with his men to—their house. The Chas had committed suicide. My father searched the place thoroughly. The Necklace was gone. And the child, of course, was gone, too. There was no cure for her, you see, Mr. Auden. I had always assumed she was dead—until now."

"So now she's back. Seventeen years old, and alive, and looking for the Necklace."

He gave his version of a nod again.

I could have filled in the rest for him. In the Asian community, all this month, word had gone around that Chamic followers of the death goddess were in London, that they were searching for something they had lost. And the trail was fourteen years cold, so the people in this house had simply armed themselves and lain low and hoped that the others would search and fail and go away. At first that had seemed to be the case; they were safe. Until tonight, when someone had turned up at Scully's workshop claiming to be a journalist, asking after a certain Mrs. Cha—and the man in the wheelchair had ordered me put out of the way, assuming I was with the *kalai*. Assuming I was working for them.

Which, in a way, I was.

I squatted in that empty, echoing room and gazed into his face. The hideousness of it. Like a bust formed, not in marble, but in mutilated putty. *And in the dream, the child struggled, the blanket fell away from its face. I looked into its face.*

If I listened very carefully, I could hear the house settling gently around me. A creak of timber here, a rattle from the old slate roof. The man's tortured eyes had closed now; his crooked mouth was open slightly with exhaustion.

I swallowed, painfully.

"The girl? What if she gets to the Necklace?"

"She will—sooner or later. With—or without you. Her elder followers are—adepts of the ways of the *kalai*. She herself—has been groomed for—the role of priestess since childhood. And the death and destruction in London, the presence of Kali herself, has fed them, made them strong. Very strong, Mr. Auden. Perhaps enough—to tap into some portion of the magic, make great spells in the seeking and finding of lost objects. They must be desperate enough now to risk that even without the Necklace. When she finds it—she will become Kali incarnate on Earth. And she might not return to Asia, Mr. Auden. She might look on what she sees here, find it good."

There were gentle, shuffling footsteps in the hallway.

"You really do believe all that?"

"Yes." His eyelids seemed to flutter with slight amusement. "But you, of course, do not.

"There is one way," he said, gazing into his own darkness, "we can settle these people once and for all."

"Uh-huh?"

"Where are they, Mr. Auden? Where are—the *kalai*?"

"In Hampstead," I said. "Somewhere there. I don't know."

"And their temple?"

I paused, thinking about the child's face.

"Somewhere in Hampstead as well, I think."

He appeared quite satisfied, did not seem to sense that I was lying. "We have our own contacts, Mr. Auden. I should say we will find them in the next forty-eight hours, and when we do . . ." Something like a smile tugged up the edges of his lips. "Go home, Mr. Auden. This is no longer your affair. Go home."

There must have been a buzzer fitted into the arm of his wheelchair, because a moment later the door opened and one of the young men came striding in, pistol hanging at his side.

"Tian?" the man in the wheelchair said. "Mr. Auden is leaving us now. He is to be allowed free passage, unharmed. Is that understood?"

The young man nodded. He began to precede me to the door.

"Oh, Tian!" the wheelchair man called out. "I have something—for Mr. Auden. In my left pocket here. Take it out—and give it to him."

It was a small yellow diamond, cut very flat, the edges of the facets glimmering in my palm. I regarded the man quizzically.

"The eye of a statue," he explained, "from one—of the Bon temples in Tibet. It was taken from there, so I understand, by a— minor lama fleeing from the communist Chinese, who fell foul of *dacoits* as soon as he crossed the border into India. I myself have little regard for such trinkets. But until this— threat is over you are still highly vulnerable. It may be of some help. Please take it."

I hesitated a moment. Then slipped the stone into my breast pocket. Tian preceded me as far as the front door, and after that I was, once more, alone in the night.

I went for my car.

# CHAPTER 26

Anyone stupid enough to be wandering out that night would have seen a large gray-green sedan flash by, jump the red lights at the crossroads and dwindle to invisibility along the damp, unyielding road; that stupid person would probably curse the driver for a fool, shrug, and walk away. The police were too busy that night to bother with one speeding car, so I was allowed to play the fool. The few remaining lights of central London lit my progress as I drove. The gun was heavy in my pocket. My throat burned with the need for alcohol. I tried to ignore it, stared past my windshield, past the wipers, at the point where my headlamp beams diminished against the darkness.

And all the while, my mind was turning

over, over. Peter Kyznik, hanged. How had she worked on him? He had ended up a drug addict, so it could not have been too difficult. Stuart Rawlinson? The gambling? The poverty it brought, and the promise of some easy money if the jewelry was found?

Sandy Mallory? Well, I had already worked that out.

And myself . . .

*"I think you are still a good journalist,"* she said.

*"You're wrong."*

*"The way you said you simply want to know. You would go to the ends of the Earth to fulfill that simple wish."*

To the ends of the bloody Earth.

I found myself thinking about the Chas, how totally they could have vanished as illegal immigrants. Probably had some money when they started out, and had it bled from them by all the parasites and sharks along the way. Probably ended up not even knowing which country in the West they would arrive in. Impossible to trace. Unless, of course, you got somebody with foreknowledge and connections to do the tracing for you.

Except that it still didn't quite make sense.

America? How the hell had she ended up in America?

The National Westminster tower was lurching to the right of me by now; I was leaving central London and the business district, sliding on to the main road eastward. It was three forty-seven by the time I reached the docks.

K. J. GOPALI said the name on the warehouse door.

The bright red transit van was parked outside.

I killed all the lights, allowed the car to idle to a halt in the shadows across the way. The front door of the warehouse was slightly open this time; there was a pale, flickering suggestion of a light coming from inside. I waited. God, how many of them were in there? Was she there? I slid the gun from my pocket, spun the chamber, and quietly got out. I seemed to make no sound at all, crossing the cobbled foreyard; that *had* to be my imagination. I seemed to be floating. When I reached the iron door, I paused another moment, listening, and then slipped inside.

There were four of them, including her.

The temple was exactly as it had been. The wooden gallery overhead, running the entire perimeter. The tapestries below them, designed with flowers and thorned blooms, curling from the mouths of stylized monsters. The candles ranked on either side. And just beyond the light of the candles ... four of them, their backs to me, standing at the altar of that dancing, deranged goddess. There was another dead animal lying on the slab. A long curved sword, much like the one that had killed Sandy Mallory, lay beside it, reflecting the candlelight.

They were totally engrossed in their work at the altar. Slicing patterns in the goat with small, very bright knives. Picking up rattles and shaking them. Murmuring chants so guttural they sounded barely human.

The wheelchair man had been right. They were no longer simply worshiping, as they had been doing the first time I'd visited the temple—they were actually trying to *conjure*, reach in and extract some substance, some magic, from a belief as old as history itself. I had led them most of the way. They were seriously hoping their own bizarre mythology could do the rest.

*They are crazy—*

The wind was there in the temple again.

*Crazy!*

It was moaning along the inner walls, fluttering the curtains, just as before.

Yet, how strange—how *strange*—the wind did not disturb the heavy pall of candle smoke above the altar. There was the smell of incense, claustrophobic on the air.

Something inside of me tugged and pleaded, urging me to get out of there.

The smoke seemed to thicken, its surfaces roiling.

I glanced at it once more. I had not come

here for that. I glanced once more at the
supplicants by their altar, steadied myself.

And I thought about the figures clustered
around the dying woman on the slab. I
thought about the dream.

"In the dream—" I said, very loudly.

All four of them spun around, she with her
fists clenched tightly by her sides. One of the
others was holding one of those bronze bowls
full of blood. I could not see any of their
faces. But they could see me, and my gun.

"In the dream," I repeated, quieter, "we
stopped the jeep and went inside the *dinh*.
The people of Sam Loong were clustered
around their dying priestess. They had their
backs turned, and they didn't see us. Stuart
got ready to take a shot. The Chas were
there, in full ceremonial dress, holding the
two-year-old daughter between them. She
was completely covered with a blanket, to
hide her from sight. But it was hot, and I
suppose she didn't like that, so she struggled,
and the blanket fell away, and we saw her
face."

The pall of smoke was huge. . . .

"Stuart gasped. He fumbled and dropped
the camera, and in that enclosed space it
sounded like a boulder, falling. Everyone
heard. Everyone saw us. We had violated
their holy place, we had defiled their shrine.
The ones at the front came at us, but we got
back to the jeep ahead of them, and sped

away. And then we hit the land mine, half a mile down the road. I think I can fill in what happened next."

*... massive ...*

"The helicopter got to us and carried us away before the Sam Loong people reached us. Once we were in the hospital, there was no way to get near us. But our *names*, that was a different matter. Someone managed to get hold of them, someone even managed to get into the hospital, steal our identity cards. But after that, we were shipped to Saigon, and then out of Vietnam for good. If we'd have stayed, we'd have been dead men.

"Then fifteen years pass, and it turns out lucky you didn't kill us after all, because the Chas are gone and the Necklace is gone, and the only solid lead you have, over the tangle of all those years, are the names of four middle-aged journalists who might have seen something useful in that *dinh* in Vietnam, might remember something which'll lead you to your goal. It's slim, but it's all you've got; so you work through Mallory and Kyznik and Rawlinson, and they're no use at all. You kill them and cover your tracks. You come finally to me—and I used to be one of the best journalists a person could imagine, so you feed me a few hints, just enough to get me going, and then turn me loose to sift through the debris of a decade and a half and untangle the trail and find the Necklace for you.

"And—shall I tell you something? The trail stopped half an hour ago. It went and petered out to a dead end. I can't remember anything useful. I can't find your Necklace for you. It's been a game, and it's over."

The wind snatched my last words, made them echo against the temple walls.

*over . . . over . . . over . . .*

That inner tugging, pleading, would not go away. There was something terrible present in this foul place. Something which my subconscious was cringing from, though my conscious mind could not detect it.

The smoke—*keep your mind on the Chams, laddie, they still have those damned knives, I never heard them drop*—the smoke filled the whole upper edge of my vision, opaque enough now to change the quality of light in the temple, cast shadows as vast and bottomless as night.

Fighting the urge to turn and run, I motioned with my revolver.

The wind rose in strength to a howling.

"Move into the light!" I shouted above it to the four silhouettes. I had to get them out of here, to the police. And more—I had to uncover the final link, get down to the truth. "Come on! Now! Move where I can see you!"

The wind was flapping at their ancient garments now. The ball of smoke writhed wildly. All four of them began walking, very slowly, into the glow of the main sets of candles. Three were older Chamic men; I had seen them before as part of the puppet theater.

And the woman . . .

Standing between her followers, enmeshed at first in the shadows they cast, hers were the very last set of features to resolve.

But finally, the glow of twice a dozen candles danced across her face.

And then I knew. Then I understood. I had the truth.

The Cham holding the bronze bowl dropped it. Blood splattered in a vivid explosion almost to my feet.

And in that instant, the truth was no longer simply mine. I felt the wind rip it from my head, bear it upward. That shrieking, it transformed to an insane, inhuman gibbering.

The smoke began to coalesce.

It began to take on a new form.

God knew what kept me on my feet. I fired two shots into it, completely without effect.

You can't kill *that*! Kill the followers! Kill the believers!

They were already moving, scattering, back into the shadows, their knives glinting. Sheer panic made my aim straighter, truer, than it should have been. I caught, first, the elder who had dropped the bowl, took him with one bullet through the chest. The impact lifted him and carried him six inches, dropped him in a tangled, ghastly heap against the foot of the altar. The others were running. The woman ... the girl ... I could not see her!

The smoke was still drawing in on itself. Gigantic, a torso was already forming, head and arms were realized, but vaguely.

*Concentrate.*

The wind blew a stand of candles over. It fell against the tapestry, and the edges of the cloth began to blaze. More smoke filled the air. The entrance to the warehouse was still open. I could make my escape now. But— that *thing* knew what I knew, the route to the Necklace, could pass the knowledge on to the *kalai*, and their new priestess, and when they had it—she might look on what she sees here, find it good, the man in the wheelchair had said.

I shot the second man as he was ducking behind a curtain. He was quite visible now in the rapidly spreading fire, and as he died his hands spasmed, clawed, a section of tapestry came rending slowly down with him. His limbs twitched as he hit the floor, but that was only shattered reflexes, he was finished. The third was already on the stairs to the upper gallery, practically out of sight. I tried to track him between the wooden railings. But he was gone. Up there. Somewhere.

I looked back toward the altar. The sword had been taken.

My eyes searched the shadows, trying to find a hint of that girl, a flash of steel. At first, there was nothing. Then I thought I saw something move, edged gently forward.

I could feel that third man on the gallery above me, hear him clambering over the railings, and I swung around to see his face looming above me—*and a far larger figure looming above that*. A knife was in his hand, all right. He jumped, was rushing down toward me, and somehow I must have managed to squeeze off a shot, since, as we both went down together, he was no more than a dead limp weight on top of me.

The revolver spun out of my grasp.

A massive, ultimately dark shadow crept over me. . . .

I craned my head up, screamed.

There it was.

Black as all the deaths since time began. Featureless as smooth, night-colored stone. Formed out of the smoke of humanity's billion funeral pyres, and fashioned by the winds of hell. Its four horrible arms writhed serpentinely. Reached down toward me.

And suddenly stopped.

My eyes went where the smoke-thing seemed to be looking. Something small and bright glowed on the floor. It was the yellow diamond. The eye of the Tibetan statue. A tiny, steady voice seemed to be coming from it. I gazed at it and there, caught within its translucent depths, was the image of the crippled Vietnamese in his wheelchair. Heaven knew with what effort, he had raised his arms to his face, tented his fingers in front of him, was reciting a mantra.

The smoke-thing reached toward the offending article, recoiled as though from heat, reared back.

Then it began sucking toward the far end of the temple, where the light of the flames had revealed the girl's motionless figure, the sword held out in front of her. Her mouth was open in a soundless yell. It was into that which the smoke-thing poured, contracting, swarming endlessly in, until it filled her.

Her eyes incandesced, a bright, hot carnelian. She began to run toward me.

Everything seemed fractured, seemed to quiver and leap, spinning with oranges and reds and yellows. The riots again; Vietnam within the confines of four smoking walls. I had been thrown from the jeep again, couldn't move below the waist. The injury to my leg and the weight of the dead man on me combined, I began to black out. *No!* I shook my head, stretched, gazing at not the gun but its reflection in the Tibetan diamond. *Concentrate!*

You should have died fifteen years ago, a voice in my head seemed to say. Now you *will* die.

*Concentrate!*

She gives life, only to take it away again.

*Concentrate!*

My hand closed around cold metal.

I propped myself up on both elbows, knowing that there was only one full chamber left in the revolver.

The girl was almost on me.

She swung the sword back across her shoulder.

Then brought it scything forward and down, toward my neck.

And the blade flashed as it came.

And time stretched to infinity.

And the gun went off between my hands.

I don't remember much of what happened when the girl went flailing back. But as she crashed against the floor, her mouth opened, and smoke came pouring out in one continuous stream, somehow piercing a hole through the temple roof and vanishing.

Then the incandescence went from her eyes. They glazed over, finally became dull. I found the strength to push the dead man from me, hobble to my feet, limp across.

The flames had covered most of a wall by now, but I stayed there as long as I could, looking down at her face. I should have guessed. Sandy Mallory, his love for beautiful women. I really should have guessed. Even in death she held a radiance, like a delicate light beneath her smooth, translucent skin, her fine bone structure, pretty as an orchid bud. I should have guessed.

Not the real "priestess expectant" at all. Not the daughter of a goddess. Just a refugee girl who'd been brought up by her elders to be more than that. Quite insane. Quite fake in terms of her own culture. A pretender.

A spark fluttered down onto her dress and began to take light. I went away from that place.

"You're the first visitor she's ever had," said the assistant matron.

It was three days later. It had taken me that long to trace the hospital. A lot had happened in that time, and most of it had been reported in the newspapers. Such as the massacre—headlined as a gangland deed—of fourteen Chams and Asians in a house on the borders of Hampstead. The wheelchair man had kept his promise. Not one of the Sam Loong people had gotten away. The other five were community leaders, each wearing a medallion with the sign of the *kalai* engraved on it. Peter Singh was among them. And, of course, the papers had tried to tie that slaughter in with the discovery of four charred bodies in the burning dockside warehouse.

They were not the only ones to make the connection—Grey had hauled me in for six hours, the day before last, but I had smiled and looked blank, and he had finally let me go. And the riots had stopped; petered out into isolated skirmishes, then silence. "*She is here*," Peter had said. I watched the assistant matron precede me in her starched white uniform.

By the massive window looking out onto the countryside, children and teenagers played as best they could. Some of them—bringing back recent memories—were in wheelchairs. Others made the ones in wheelchairs look like the lucky ones.

"It sounds rather barbaric," said the assistant matron, "but we keep her in the east wing, away from the other children." She led me down a maze of corridors painted white and yellow. "How old was she when you last saw her?"

"Two," I said.

"That's about right. The symptoms of the disease become apparent about that time."

She gave me a brief history of how the child had been found abandoned, been shunted from one institution to another until she had ended up here. By the time she had finished, we had reached the appropriate door. She opened it, and we both stood in the gap.

There were huge windows, staring out

across a hillside and a copse of trees. There were pictures of elephants and clowns taped to the walls, and toys piled in the corner. At the center of the room, motionless, her back to us, sat a small girl in a hospital smock. There was something wrong, I could already see, with the shape of her skull, with the curve of her spine.

"Katie," the assistant matron said, very softly.

The child turned slowly around. I caught a glimpse of her face. Then I was closing my eyes, and turning away, and murmuring *Oh, God*, and biting my tongue to try and stop the nausea. It took me almost a minute to manage to look back.

My eyes were watering. "What's wrong with her?" I asked.

"We call it Hurler's syndrome. The common term is 'gargoylism.'"

"Is it—mental as well as physical?"

"Completely. She's seventeen years old. She wears diapers, she can't talk, she can't even bathe herself."

Something glittered around the child's throat. It was a polished bronze necklace, formed out of a chain of tiny metal skulls. They smiled, the way all skulls do. Topaz eyes glinted out at me.

"She's dying, even now," the assistant matron told me. "They don't last much beyond adolescence, you know. In a few short months, there will be no more Katie. And perhaps, for her, that will be a blessing. You're the only outsider who's even had the remotest connection with her. Is there anything you want done?"

I bunched my shoulders together and tried to steady my breathing.

"When she . . . goes, will she be cremated?"

"Yes."

"Leave the necklace with her," I heard myself say. "That's all."

Not much later, I found myself out on the gravel forecourt, shivering against the fresh, cold air. My car was parked a little farther down the drive. I began walking toward it. And stopped, and turned. Katie had come to her window and was staring out at me, sad brown eyes trapped in that ruin of a face. She didn't know who I was, who she was, what the world was. She was just a child with her mind largely hollow, and all that she could do was listen to the echoes in that empty space, and stare. Some fates, all told, are far worse.

"Good-bye, Jagadgauri," I whispered.

Then I drove back to the city.

*More compulsive fiction from Headline:*

# BAIT
# OF LIES

## HARDIMAN SCOTT
## AND BECKY ALLAN

**The tense political thriller of intrigue and treachery**

Carolyn Hailston's student trip to Prague becomes a nightmare when she and her Czech lover are arrested by the security police. To ensure Josef's freedom, she must agree to collaborate with the Czech secret service on her return to England. No one would call Carolyn a promising recruit, except for one thing – her father is a government minister with access to secrets that can rock the delicate balance of power in Europe.

At home, her amateur attempts at espionage bring Carolyn swiftly to the notice of spymaster David Rackham. But her naive involvement in the politics of power and treachery only marks the entrance to a labyrinth of blackmail, murder and corruption that will endanger her own life, threaten her father's career, and bring the government to the brink of an international crisis of terrifying proportions . . .

**FICTION**   0-7472-3008-0   **£2.50**

WINNER OF THE WORLD FANTASY AWARD

# Dan Simmons

# SONG of KALI

Calcutta – a monstrous city of slums, disease and misery, clasped in the fetid embrace of an ancient cult.

Kali – the dark mother of pain, four-armed and eternal, her song the sound of death and destruction.

Robert Luczak – caught in a vortex of violence that threatens to engulf the entire world in an apocalyptic orgy of death.

The song of Kali has just begun . . .

"*Song of Kali* is as harrowing and ghoulish as anyone could wish. Simmons makes the stuff of nightmare very real indeed."
*Locus*

0 7472 3044 7    £2.95

Headline books are available at your book-shop or newsagent, or can be ordered from the following address:

Headline Book Publishing PLC
Cash Sales Department
PO Box 11
Falmouth
Cornwall
TR10 9EN
England

UK customers please send cheque or postal order (no currency), allowing 60p for postage and packing for the first book, plus 25p for the second book and 15p for each additional book ordered up to a maximum charge of £1.90 in UK.

BFPO customers please allow 60p for postage and packing for the first book, plus 25p for the second book and 15p per copy for the next seven books, thereafter 9p per book.

Overseas and Eire customers please allow £1.25 for postage and packing for the first book, plus 75p for the second book and 28p for each subsequent book.